BUILDING HOME

An Eastern Shore Romance

DEE ERNST

To find more of Dee's books, go to
www.deeernst.com

Comments? Questions? An uncontrollable desire to just chat? You can reach me at
Dee@deeernst.com

ISBN - 9780998506883

❀ Created with Vellum

Chapter One

I 'd never been much of a risk taker.

I was a good girl in high school. I dated a nice, quiet boy, a few years older than I, who invariably apologized after we had sex because I didn't scream out loud when I had an orgasm. It wasn't his fault, because, although I never told him, I never really *had* an orgasm, despite all his efforts. He was such a great guy that I didn't want to disappoint him. Maybe if I had offered a suggestion or two, or maybe even moved his hand to the right spot, things would have worked out differently. But like I said, I didn't take risks, and I was not going to seem pushy or sexually aggressive because he might break up with me, and *then* where would I be?

That was my life. My whole life. Lots of things happened between then and now, but...

Now I stood, gazing at my cell phone at pictures of a rather dilapidated house that my old college roommate was trying to talk me into.

Buy it, she said.

It's a great investment, she said.

It's right on Main Street in Cape Edwards, and you can walk to all the bars and restaurants, as well as the beach, she said.

You could open a real estate office right in town.

Or do something completely different.

Or take the money from your mom's estate and just be a lady of leisure.

You could start your life all over.

Begin a new second act.

And you've been here before and you always say you love it. And do you remember all the hot men?

I didn't, actually. And to be honest, hot men were not a priority. Over a year ago I'd broken up with Daniel, my boyfriend of eleven years, to care for my mother. I discovered that my life hummed along just fine without him in it. Based on that, I pretty much decided that if being unattached for the rest of my natural life was going to be a thing, it was *not* going to be the end of the world.

I flipped through the pictures again. It was a cute little house, just two bedrooms, with a wide front porch. Inside, walls were sagging and the kitchen was impossible. There wasn't a picture of the bathroom, which I knew was not a very good sign. But it was all workable. Even the sad looking little backyard had great potential, with some pavers and a few potted plants. I could have a dog.

I'd never had a dog before. My first husband was a cat person, Daniel had been allergic, and I had spent most of the past two years spending all my nonworking hours caring for my mother, who was slowly wasting away from cancer, which left no time to devote to a pet. Or to Daniel, come to that.

I'd been selling houses in Rehoboth, Delaware for almost twenty-five years, and I was good at it. But I had never owned my own home. When I married Martin, my ex-husband, I moved into his condo right from my parents' house. After the divorce, I went back to Mom's. Then, I moved in with Daniel. Then, I moved back in with Mom after she got sick.

Finally, my own house.

Right on Main Street.

Close to bars and restaurants.

With all those hot men...

Why the hell not?

I thought about it for almost a month, during which time I settled my mother's estate and tried to find a way to live comfortably in *her* house.

I couldn't. It would always be her house, not mine.

I finally did the work and realized how much it was worth.

Holy crap.

I looked at those pictures again. It was selling for dirt-cheap because the interior needed so much work, like a brand new kitchen and bathroom, paint...a major rehab job. Terri, in her original text had mentioned something about the perfect guys to help with the renovation, and how we could flip the property and become HGTV stars.

Terri got carried away with some of her ideas, but if she already knew who would help with the renovation...

Sold! I texted her.

Terri's return text was a series of emoji. Then, of course, she called.

"Oh, Chris, this is going to be so much fun! You can stay with me and we can walk to the job site every day."

"Terri," I warned her, "you have somebody to do the renovations, right?"

"Yes. The McCann brothers. Steve McCann and I have, if I can brag just a little, a certain chemistry. I know that once he and I start working together, things will really start to take off. He's a bit younger than I am, but that's fine. What's a five-year difference at our age?'"

"So...you want me to buy this house so you can hit on some *guy*?"

"Of course not. I want you to buy this house because every time you've come down here, you've had a great time."

That was true.

"And you've had a rough couple of years with your mom. You've lived in the same place your whole life, Chris, and could use a change of scenery."

That was also true.

"Change is good for the soul. Don't you feel like you need to shake things up? Now is your chance."

I sighed. "You're right. Let's do this. I guess I can drive down there for the sale, but I have to close the office up here, and that's going to take a while. Can you buy this for me?"

"Of course."

"Okay then. I'll send you a power of attorney, wire you the cash, and we can get going."

She squealed. Fifty-year-old women should not squeal, but that's Terri for you.

"Oh, Chris, I am so excited. And you know what the best part is?"

I was smiling over the phone. "That you and I will be able to walk to each other's houses every day?"

"No, I meant, beside that. Steve McCann has an older brother. His name is Mike, and he has a beard, and he's closer to our age, and I know the two of you would be perfect together." She clicked off the phone before I could yell WTF?

As a point of information, I eventually married that nice, quiet high school boy, and I eventually had an orgasm. But not with him.

Cape Edwards was a quiet little town on the Eastern Shore of Virginia, just north of the Chesapeake Bay Bridge, and Terri lived in a condo right on Main Street, conveniently over a wine and cheese shop. She was the postmistress at the Eastville, VA post office, which suited her very well because she loved gossip. She wasn't mean-spirited or even all that nosy. She had a real interest in people, all sorts of people. When we were in college, and hung out in bars, she could get total strangers who had originally intended to try for a quickie to tell her their entire life story instead. She did not have a mean bone in her body, had a warm, generous heart and a deep, loving soul, and we had been friends for over thirty years.

Which is why I trusted her.

I also knew her well enough to detect even the tiniest sliver of BS. So when she told me things, I knew what to accept and what to push aside for further evaluation.

My mother had died just after the new year. It took a few months to find a buyer for Mom's house and negotiate the sale of my interest in the real estate office to my partners. I felt I had rid myself of all the baggage, emotional and actual. I felt free and supremely confident. Terri had found me the perfect house, it was in an almost perfect little town, and I was starting a grand adventure. I packed my car, attached a little U-Haul trailer for my books and mementos, and drove south.

The last time I'd been in Cape Edwards, almost two years ago, I'd gotten very drunk. It wasn't my fault. I had just found out that my mother had pancreatic cancer, and the prognosis was not good. Terri Coburn, who had held my hand many times while we were college juniors and seniors at the University of Delaware, took me to a place called Sam's on Main, where the bartender, upon hearing my sad story, started poring shots of tequila. Quite honestly, I don't remember him stopping. Tequila, by the way, was not my usual drink. In fact, I'd never *had* a usual drink. But tequila tasted just about right that night, and I do remember ending up on the beach in the middle of the night, naked, encouraging the other women who had followed me to take their clothes off as well and dive in.

It was a big night for me. As a person usually so cautious I normally wouldn't be found on the beach without three cover-ups and a striped umbrella to hide under, being naked was a real departure. As I also remember, the tide was so far out that I almost got lost trying to find actual water, prompting Terri, who had remained clothed, to trick me into turning back to shore with the promise of jerk chicken wings.

But something changed in me that night. I realized that I had spent my entire life doing the "right" thing: playing it safe and making sure I hadn't stepped on anyone's toes. And my mother was going to die, and all that good behavior wasn't going to make a bit of difference. Which is why, after she'd gone, I made a decision to try to live my life differently—take the chance, do the unexpected, step out in a different direction. Buying a house, sight unseen, was a big first step. But now I found myself reining in a little. All that courage and bravado seemed to shrink back as I left the place I'd called home for most of my life and headed south.

As I remembered, summers were hot on the Delmarva Peninsula, but at least Cape Edwards had a bit of a breeze. I drove down State Road 31 until it curved west toward the Chesapeake Bay. I'd been down this road before. I'd been visiting Terri in Cape Edwards since we were in college together, and she invited me to spend a week at the house her family rented every year. This was familiar territory to me, and I slowed down as I came to where I thought my new house was, just at the beginning of Main Street.

There it was, looking forlorn and unhappy with its unkempt yard and sagging porch. On one side of it was a neat little bungalow, surrounded by a white picket fence. On the other side was a vacant lot, one of several on this end of town, with a stand of four or five pines trees and patches of weeds growing in the dense shade. And across the street...that had been an empty lot as well, where, for years, old railroad freight cars had sat rusting. Now it was a bustling construction site, the foundation laid for what looked to be four or five separate retail spaces. I slowed to get a closer look. What was going on across the street from my new house? At least I thought it was better than rusting junk, which I was sure was home to critters I didn't care to think about.

I drove farther down Main Street, and the small houses gave way to brick-front shops and restaurants. Cape Edwards hadn't gotten sleek and modern. There were no high-rises or fancy waterfront hotels. It was still quaint and small and charming. I turned into the alleyway that ran behind all the shops. Terri had a single parking spot right behind her apartment but also rented space in a neighbor's yard on the opposite side of the alley. She usually kept her golf cart there but told me I could pull in and use the space. I did, got out and stretched, feeling the breeze, smelling the salt air. This, I knew, was going to be just what I needed. A fresh start.

Terri given me the code to the back door lock, so I sent her a quick text that I'd arrived. I got a heart emoji back from her as I let myself in and up, one flight, to her apartment.

She threw open the door and wrapped both arms around me, picking me up off the ground and swirling me around. I'm barely five foot zilch, and she had at least six inches on me, not to mention twenty or thirty pounds. Not heavy at all, just very well rounded, with breasts that entered a room a full minute before the rest of her body.

She dropped me to the floor. "Are you tired? Oh, I hope not, because there's someone really wonderful playing at the Grove, and then we're all going out to dinner...everyone is so excited to see you again." She beamed. "And the McCann brothers are meeting us first thing tomorrow, so you can see the house, and hear what they plan to do. They are just finishing up a house for the new doctor, Dara French, and it's supposed to be amazing inside. I can't wait to hear what they're going to do to your place."

The Grove was a gallery on Main Street, and their Friday night ritual was free wine and cheese and something: a singer, a poet—a live performance of some kind. And I knew that Terri spent Friday nights cruising Main Street with her friends, all of whom I'd met before. They were a terrific bunch of women.

"Can I pee? And brush my hair? And maybe change out of my sweaty clothes?"

She waved her hand. "Of course. Give me your keys and I'll bring up a suitcase or two."

I handed them over. "Just my Vera Bradley thing in the back seat, and the small suitcase." Everything else was in my U-Haul.

I watched her go, went to the bathroom, then was drawn, as I always was, to her front balcony. She overlooked all of Main Street, and the marina was right beyond. If you stuck your head out far enough and looked toward the west, you could even see the bay. This was my future, a new place called home, and I was suddenly struck by the enormity of what I'd done—left my whole life behind to start new. I took a deep breath of salty air for courage. I was doing the right thing. I was sure of it. I had to shake off the old me, the one who'd been afraid to take a chance. Besides, it was way too late to turn back now.

We hit Main Street half an hour later. Terri, at breakneck speed, brought me up-to-date on all of gossip in town. There was a new doctor, a woman from Jamaica with dreadlocks and a charming accent. Sam, who had owned Sam's on Main, died suddenly, and he had a son that no one had ever known about who had taken over the bar and moved in with Jenna, Sam's ex-wife, who I knew was one of Terri's friends.

"Jenna, of course, was apoplectic," Terri explained. "And hurt. She and Sam were friends, and for him to never tell her he had a son...well, anyway, he, that is, Craig, showed up with his three daughters and moved in! Sam had owned half the house, but Jenna always imagined that his half would go to her. I mean, why wouldn't she?"

"Wait—she and Sam were divorced, right?"

"Yes, but Sam always kept his half of the house. He used to joke that when he got old and feeble he'd move back in, and Jenna would have to take care of him! I'm gonna miss Sam, he was such a hoot. Anyway—Craig moves in, and he's a dead ringer for Sam when Sam was *much* younger, so of course, Jenna has all sorts of very complicated and if I may say, lustful thoughts. It's a mess."

"Jenna is the redhead? The nurse? She struck me as someone who wouldn't take something like that sitting down."

"Well, she was in a real corner, legally speaking. Poor Jenna."

"Does she still have the goats?"

"Yes, and she's picked up another dog since you were here last. Jenna named her Bit, because we have no idea what she might be, but probably a little bit of everything. Here we are."

I'd never been down here during the summer months, and Terri had always told me that the summer people tended to take over the town. By the number of people in the space, I could see she was right. The room was crowded, and everyone was dressed in summer finery: long sleeveless dresses and linen shirts, not the usual jeans-and-T-shirt crowd of off-season.

"Let me get us some wine," Terri said. "Just stay here."

Last time I had been here, it had been in mid-May, and there weren't any crowds. I'd lived my whole life in a beach town, and I knew what the summers were like. They were absolute hell, that's what they were like. There was traffic and loud, obnoxious children everywhere; you couldn't get into your favorite restaurant or bars...I hated summers. But, I told myself that Cape Edwards was much smaller. And the official season was only four months out of the year. Its attraction was the Chesapeake Bay, not the ocean. This wasn't a place for college kids to hang out or where Millennials rented a place for the whole season. This was a summer spot where families and couples came back year after year.

Terri practically had to wrestle her way back to me, but resourceful as she is, looked like she hadn't spilled a drop of wine. "Jenna and Karen are over there. I'll run interference."

I followed Terri, keeping my head down and my hand over the top of the wine glass, to reduce the chance of spillage.

Jenna and Karen both had hugs. Jenna Ferris was a redhead, pale skinned, freckled and slender. Karen Helfman was older, closer to my age, with wiry hair gone completely gray, dark eyes in a tanned and wrinkled face, and a killer body. She was a yoga instructor, and every time I'd met her I thought it might be worth giving yoga a try if my body could look like hers, instead of it looking like...well, not toned and tight with arms that Tina Turner could envy. I was built more along the lines of the Pillsbury Doughgirl—softer, rounder, and definitly *not* toned.

It was good to see them, and I felt grateful that I wasn't moving to a place where I'd be a total stranger. I'd left behind friends in Rehoboth, but many had been Daniel and my friends, and after the split had drifted away. There were plenty of people there I'd known since childhood, but after Mom got sick, my life became very narrow, and I kept even my oldest friends at arms length. Now, in Cape Edwards, I had Terri and a circle of *her* friends that I could gradually get to know better, and hopefully some of them would become my friends as well.

"She just drove down this second," Terri explained, grinning. "She's staying with me, and tomorrow she's seeing the house for the first time. Want to meet us?"

Jenna smiled. "Sure. But Chris, you haven't seen the house at all? And you let Terri buy it for you?"

"I saw the pictures on Zillow," I explained.

Terri gave me a big squeeze. "We're going to have so much fun!"

Karen shook her head at me. "You let her talk you into this?"

I shrugged my shoulders. "I really needed the change, and I was swayed by the promise of hot men."

"And you believed *Terri?*" Jenna asked, still smiling

I smiled back. "I've known her along time, so I've learned to sift out the BS. I really just want to live somewhere I can walk to both the water and at least one bar."

"Well, then your new place is perfect," Jenna said.

I rolled my eyes. "Not yet, but I see potential."

Terri started introducing me to people. Sadly, none of them had nametags, and after a few minutes my brain started to short circuit.

"I can't remember a single person I've met since that short blond man. Stu."

She shook her head. "Stan. Okay, let's go.

We went down the street to a place called Shorty's, then went further down to Sam's on Main. Terri got stopped right at the doorway, so I followed Jenna, who went over to the restaurant side and waved at a tall, very handsome man in conversation with a waitperson. He looked up briefly and flashed her a smile. Then he saw me, and our eyes met for just enough of a second for me to feel a smile start. Maybe Terri *wasn't* so wrong about those hot men.

I poked Jenna in the ribs. "See, sometimes Terri tells the truth."

Terri, coming up behind, grabbed my arm and shook her head. "He's taken."

"No," Jenna said distinctly, "he's not." She looked at me. "That's Craig Ferris. He owns Sam's now. He's got three girls."

I did not see that as an obstacle at all. "Not a problem."

Terri glared at her and Jenna glared back. Obviously, I was missing something completely, so I blindly turned to the person next to me, with a mind to start a casual conversation. Sadly, it was a much younger man, obviously very drunk, who was trying to look down the front of my dress from his considerable height.

Karen came to the rescue, grabbed my arm and pulled me away, waving politely at the drunk.

"Done here," I yelled in her ear. She nodded in agreement, tapped Terri on the shoulder, and we all walked further down Main Street.

We finally found an outside table in front of Bogey's. At this point, the trip was getting to me, the crowd was getting to me, the noise was absolutely getting to me, so I ordered tequila shots all around, feeling there was a certain symmetry. I'd done this the last time I was in Cape Edwards, and now that I was back...

After the third, I felt positively giddy. I pointed to the darkness further down Main Street. "See? I'm going to be living right there. Close to everything."

"Including all this crowd walking past your house day and night," Karen said. "You'll have drunks puking on your front lawn all summer."

I hadn't thought of that. "Really?" I looked around at all the people on the sidewalk. I knew that, less than a mile from here, was a large resort, complete with town homes, condos, a marina and a pier. And that people walked back there from Main Street or rode in their golf carts. All those happy revelers, drunk and singing, yelling and whooping it up, all going right past my new house...

"It's crazy here," Stella said. "Summer is crazy. Maybe not as bad as Rehoboth, but it gets intense. But it's worth it for the rest of the year."

I sighed. "Too late now," I said, and took another shot.

Jenna grinned at me. "You keep buying rounds like this, you're going to find yourself with a lot of best friends."

Karen leaned over and whispered. "Make sure you stop. We don't want another naked romp on the beach."

"There's nothing wrong with an occasional naked romp on the beach," I declared loudly, causing a few folks from neighboring tables to look over.

Terri patted the back of my hand. "That was quite unlike you," she said.

I nodded. "Yes, it was."

"You're usually not that...uninhibited," she continued.

"No, I'm not." At least, I hadn't been then. The new and hopefully improved Chris might very well take all her clothes off and run into the Chesapeake Bay again...but, it would still have to be in the dead of night with no one around to see.

Jenna leaned across the table. "Does Cape Edwards bring out a whole other side of you?" Jenna asked.

I stared at my empty shot glass and decided enough was enough. "God, I hope so." I was actually feeling very relaxed and a bit silly. There was nothing to feel sorry or sad about. All of that was behind me, and as I looked ahead, I had no job, no responsibility...just an empty house that was not fit to live in.

"I'm not going to be sorry about this, am I?" I begged Terri.

She waved a hand. "Pish."

"Pish? Is that it? Terri, that's not even a real *word*." It may have been the tequila, but panic was setting in. That deep breath of salty air that had given me courage before was all gone, and the excitement of the drive down was melting into exhaustion, and there might be strangers puking on the front porch of my new house...

Karen put her arm around my shoulders. "We're with you, Chris. Don't worry."

Jenna nodded from across the table. "That's right. Whatever mess Terri got you into, we'll help you get out."

Terri beamed. "See? Oh, stop worrying. Everything will be just fine."

So why was I not relieved?

We made it back to Terri's around one, and I fell into bed and was instantly asleep. Then, just three minutes later, I was rudely awakened.

"Come on, girlfriend. We need to get some breakfast. On a regular Saturday, we'd be down having bacon and eggs with the girls at the Pharmacy, but today is special. We meet the McCann brothers at ten." Right. Saturday breakfast with her friends was a ritual.

"What time is it?" I mumbled.

"Time to get up and shower. You smell like you rolled in salt and limes. Lucky for you, I love salt and limes." God, had she always been this cheerful in the morning?

She was cooking eggs and bacon when I finally emerged from the bathroom, hair still in a towel. She pointed with her spatula. "Sit. Toast is coming. Want to eat outside?"

I waited until she filled my plate, then went on to the balcony. The street was already getting crowded. It was just the end of June. I could only imagine how busy things would get by July.

"How much worse does this get?" I asked Terri when she joined me.

She looked down into the street. "Actually, this is about it. Logistically speaking, there is only so much physical space here in Cape Edwards, and we're about maxed out now." She settled across from me at the wrought-iron table. "How's your head?"

I had to think. I felt pretty good unless I opened my eyes really wide..."Okay. I seem to drink a lot more than usual when I'm down here."

"Well, that's because you're usually on vacation. And tequila shots are the official drink of Cape Edwards. Once the idea that you *live* here sinks in, the urge to celebrate every night will go away. Trust me. When I first moved down here, I was looped for the first six months."

"But you had always vacationed here."

She nodded and dipped her toast in the eggs, breaking the soft yolks. "Yep. My parents brought me down every summer, so after I graduated, I just applied for every job I could find. When the post office called, I jumped at the chance. Government pension, all those days off..." She sighed. "I've really loved living here. And I've met wonderful people." She suddenly grinned. "And now you're here. Come on and eat up. We have places to be."

When we left the condo, she checked her watch. "Okay. Let's walk normally, and see how long it takes." That was harder than it should have been, because it seemed that every other person we saw wanted to talk to Terri, but she brushed them off with a smile, and soon we were past Bogey's, my little house coming up on the left.

We walked up from the marina, further away from the bay. As we neared the house, I was again struck by how large the new construction seemed to be.

"Am I going to be living across from a mall?" I asked.

She shook her head. "No. It's going to be beautiful. Believe me, I was at the planning board meeting, well, one of them, and it's going to be really well done. Just four retail spaces on the ground level and condos above. I think a bank? And maybe a craft beer place? It will be an asset."

Craft beer? An asset for Terri, maybe, but...

"Trust me," she said. "Look, there's Jenna. She'd said she'd meet us. Jenna, hi!"

Jenna, her gorgeous red hair done in a topknot, was waiting for us on the front porch. The house looked a little sadder than it had in the pictures, with a low-pitched roof, small windows on either side of a front door and a porch that had a definite droop on one side.

"Only six minutes from my condo to here," Terri told her. "I'm so excited." She took a key out of the pocket of her linen shorts and unlocked the padlock, pushed the front door open, and spread her arm out, waving me inside. "Your castle awaits."

I stepped forward eagerly. My house, my very first house...then I stopped. "Terri," I asked, not quite believing what I was seeing, "where's the floor?"

Jenna came up and peeked over my shoulder.

At some point, between the time the pictures I saw were taken and now, somebody thought it was a good idea to gut the house down to the studs, including the floor. There were floor joists running the length of the house, with narrow plywood strips laid across them, making a very scary-looking walkway.

Terri did not seem to find anything distressing about this. "We have blank slate," she said.

I took a step forward. When I did not fall, I took another. "Did you know it looked like this? Because the pictures..."

Terri, of course, had an explanation. "Well, see, the pictures on Zillow were a few years old. It had been put on the market a few years ago, hadn't sold, so the owner started to redo the place, but didn't get too far."

"So you knew there was no floor?" I asked. Surely not, I thought. Surely...

"Of course I did," Terri sounded as though I had somehow insulted her. "You don't think I'd let you buy something without my even *looking* at it."

"And, you opened the door, saw this, and decided it was just perfect for me?" I gazed upward. No ceiling. I looked ahead. There were what looked to be rooms, outlined roughly by two-by-fours.

"Chris, I told you we'd be starting from scratch. What did you think I meant? Besides, the location is ideal. I had Mike McCann look at the place, and he said the walls and the floor and roof joists are sound, and the foundation will last another hundred years. There's even a yard out back, once you cut down all the weeds and saplings. And get rid of the old tires. The point is, we can do whatever we want here."

Jenna bravely hopped on to a few of the joists, then stepped back on to the plywood path. "All of the windows are either boarded up or cracked single pane. You'll have to replace them all. The plumbing looks like at least fifty years old and the electric is knob and tube, " she informed me. Jenna, I knew, had lived alone in a big old ranch-style house, right on the Chesapeake Bay. Obviously, she knew a thing or two about houses. A whole lot more than Terri.

"What does that mean?" Terri asked.

"It means it has to go. I thought you watched HGTV," I said, trying to stay calm. I could feel the fear start to creep in, and I fought it down. All of this, I knew, could be fixed. In fact, I'd sold people houses in this kind of condition and knew that pretty much anything was possible with enough time and money. It wasn't like the place had burned to the ground, right?

Jenna was crouched down, looking at a beam. "The good news is, you can see all the beams here, and it doesn't look like you've got any termites."

"Of course not. There's not enough wood for them to eat," I muttered.

"There's lots of room, Chris. And you could have really tall ceilings." Terri pushed me toward the back of the house and spread her arms wide. "Open concept, yes? The kitchen along that wall, the dining room in that little bay window."

I was trying. I really was. "There's no window."

"No," Terri agreed, "but there will be. All we need to do is add the glass. Two bedrooms and a shared bathroom right in the back. Mike said we can move the back door out of the bedroom and to the side, and have a nice brick path to the yard. The parking pad can come right up to the house from the alley, but there's enough room for a patio."

That all sounded just dandy, but..."There's no floor. How can I live in a house with no floor?"

"You're staying with me for as long as it takes," Terri said. "Every day, you can walk down here and watch them work. And I'm taking my vacation next month, and I'm staying right here in Cape Edwards to help you out."

The BS detector began to go off. "You're staying right here in Cape Edwards so you can snag a McCann brother."

"No, honey," Terri said. "But if something should happen, that would be a real bonus."

Jenna patted me on the back. "Welcome to the neighborhood," she said.

We went further back into the house. All the windows across the back were boarded up, and it was too dark to see much. Good thing, I thought. If I got a good look at this mess, I'd probably start to cry.

"Terri, this is way more work than I imagined. How are we going to do this?"

"Hey, Terri," a voice called. "It's Steve."

I looked at Terri, who actually began to blush. Was this, then, Steve McCann, contractor extraordinaire and the object of Terri's considerable admiration? Was he going to take this broken shell of a house and turn it into something I could call home? I rolled my eyes and gingerly made my way to the front of the house.

Steve McCann was worthy of admiration, all right. He was very tall and wiry, with broad shoulders under a plain blue T-shirt. His face was all angles: a lean, jaw, thin nose, cheekbones you could cut glass with. His hair was dark and rather long, and I put him in his midforties. He was wearing jeans and had rolled-up blueprints under one arm.

He nodded to Jenna. "Hey, Red, are you in on this too?"

Jenna shook her head. "Nope. Just an innocent bystander."

I had to look way up as I stuck out my hand. "I'm Chris Polittano. I'm the official owner. Terri says you're a miracle worker."

He shook my hand slowly, and his grin was wide and showed white, even teeth. There was a lot behind that smile, but I was in no mood to try to figure any of it out.

"Well, maybe small miracles," said another man, coming up right behind Steve. "I'm Mike," he said, nodding his head. "And I promise you, we will make this place look like a dream."

Mike was just as attractive as Steve, in a completely different way. He was older, shorter, stockier, with a barrel chest. His hair was going to gray. He had a short, neat beard, and his blue eyes twinkled with humor.

I glanced at Terri, who was staring at Steve. "Walk me though it."

"Later guys," Jenna said, and carefully walked back out to the porch and was gone.

Steve looked around and sighed. "I bet you're a little discouraged by all this. It's the first time seeing the house, right?"

I nodded.

"Don't worry. We have a plan," Mike said.

Thank God, I thought. "Okay then. Show me."

Chapter Two

As it turned out, the McCann brothers knew what they were talking about.

Mike began. "First, let me tell you the story behind this house. Dave Farnham died about five years ago, and his worthless son, Dave Two, tried selling it without so much as cleaning his dad's belongings out of the closets. After a year, he took it off the market. Then, he went through the place like Sherman through Georgia, and even pulled out the appliances and the bathroom sink. Still didn't sell. Then, he got smart and called on our local architect to draw up some plans, got all his permits, and started to completely redo the place." Mike's eyes twinkled. "Well, Dave Two's wife left him, and Dave Two went on a year-long drunk. He sobered up enough to renew his permits, then got drunk again. Then, he put the house back on the market, and that's why we're all here today."

He motioned with his head. "Let's get on out to the porch so I can show you these plans without having to worry about anyone falling through the joists."

I completely agreed with his thinking, and we went out to the front porch, where we all crouched down as Steve spread the plans on the porch floor.

"Now, as you can see, this is pretty much your basic open concept with a high-end kitchen and a bath good enough for Cleopatra," Mike said.

The plan looked just fine. In fact, it was pretty much what I would have expected of a redo. Except the kitchen...

"I'd want the kitchen to be on the other side," I said. "And maybe less laundry room?"

"Ah. Well, here's the thing." Mike took a long breath. "Getting plans approved and permits in this county takes a long time. I mean, a *long* time."

Steve nodded. "Months," he said briefly.

"And Garson Heller at the zoning commission cannot be hurried. Not even for money," Mike continued. "Believe me, we've tried."

My heart sank. I did not want to wait months before work even started. I had all my stuff in a rental trailer that was rapidly becoming the world most expensive storage container.

I looked sideways at Mike. "But?"

He grinned. "Exactly. But, these plans are already approved. And we already have permits. As the new owner, if you were to take these plans *back* to the esteemed Mr. Heller and tell him how much you love them, and how you don't want to change a single thing, why, he'd probably just stamp them again and, bingo, perfectly good house plans. And we could start middle of next week."

I glanced at Terri who was, amazingly, quiet. Or maybe her tongue was glued to the roof of her mouth because Steve McCann was the kind of guy who easily caused that kind of reaction. I saw it and recognized it, but my anxiety level was such that I wasn't very susceptible.

I looked closely at the blueprints. Did it really matter what side of the house the kitchen was on? And as for that laundry room, all that extra storage space was probably a good idea. That closet in the guest room wasn't big enough, but maybe just push it out a bit? I looked up at Mike, and he read my mind.

"Now, just remember," he said, a smile playing around his lips, "that we can always tweak a few things here and there. I spoke to Susan Arnette, who drew up the plans. She's right here in town, and she said she'd be more than happy to talk with you about picking out your cabinets, flooring, all that stuff. Very creative, Susan is. And she'd also be able to make, well, *adjustments* here and there if you want."

I nodded my head. "You know what, Mike? With a few of those kinds of adjustments, these plans would be just about perfect."

"Why, Chris, I was hoping you'd say that." He picked up the blueprints, rolling them deftly into a nice bundle.

We stood. "Now, about money," I said.

The brothers exchanged a look. "Yes, well, you know that Terri here had mentioned how the two of you were going to be doing, ah..." Mike said.

"What?"

"She suggested that we act as more *guides* in the process, and you all would be doing a large portion of the work." Mike's eyes were glinting, and I could see a smile starting to form around his mouth.

I turned, very slowly, to look at Terri, who seemed totally unsurprised at Mike's statement. "We? As in, you and I?" I asked her. "Doing a large portion of the work?"

"Sure!" She seemed, as always, completely on safe ground. "We can demo and nail and paint."

I turned to the McCann brothers and smiled politely. "Please excuse us for a moment." I grabbed Terri's arm and pulled her from the porch and around to the back of the house, which was overgrown, full of junk, and infested with poison oak. It was also all mine.

"Terri," I began, "I know I said we would renovate this together, but at what point did you think we could take on a project of this magnitude? The actual demo is already done. We have now entered the construction phase. I have no experience in that, and neither do you, and I don't think nailing plywood and sawing two-by-fours are skills you can just pick up by hanging around and watching."

I took a deep breath. I had to. What had she been thinking? "When you talked about us doing this house together, I thought you meant things like putting up new moldings or hanging a new door, and maybe grouting or laying tile or painting. Speaking of which, didn't you pay someone to paint your condo when you moved in?"

She remained unbowed. "Yes, but that doesn't mean I don't know *how* to paint. Besides, Chris, *you* know all about houses."

"Yes. I know how to sell them, how to stage them, and how to hire people to fix any problems they have. I don't demo, Terri, and I don't nail. Neither do you. And there's not enough money in the world to get me on a ladder as high as I'd need to paint that ceiling."

She scrunched up her face and pointed her index finger right at my nose. "Chris, didn't you say you needed a change?"

"Yes, but—"

"And haven't you always talked about someday having a little house of your own, done up just the way *you* want?"

"Not always, just on and off—"

"And isn't Cape Edwards perfect, and isn't this location perfect, and did I not hire the best men for this job?"

I sighed. "Yes, I guess you did."

She lowered her finger. "Mike walked the house with me before I bought it, you know. It's solid. It just needs to be...filled in. You may have a point about this being, maybe, too much for us to take on, especially since I'm working and only took a week off to help. So if you say so, they can do all the real *building* part, and we can...help them. Besides," her face softened. "What else have you got to do?"

Well, she made a pretty good point there. This house was not just my future, it was pretty much all I had going on in the present day.

"Okay," I said. I looked around the back yard. There was enough junk peeking out of the waist-high weeds to fill a small dumpster. But there was also a large tree providing plenty of shade, and I could see where a side walkway would lead directly to a patio, surrounded by a low stone wall, festooned with hanging lights and potted plants. "Okay," I said again, and we walked back around to the front.

The McCann brothers, to their credit, had not gotten in their truck and driven away. The two of them were out by the curb, leaning against a battered pickup, and both straightened up when they saw us.

"What's the verdict?" Steve asked.

"Terri said you did a walkthrough," I said. "What do you find?"

"Welp." Mike passed his hand over his face. "I can tell you, you'll need all new mechanicals, new windows, a new roof and major landscape work in the back there. The porch needs new footings, so we'd just as soon tear it down and rebuild. Beyond all that, it's some framing, drywall, insulation, a new floor, kitchen, and laundry space. The good news is you only have one bathroom."

"And how much would all that would cost? *Without* any help from Terri or I?"

I looked at him. His eyes were twinkling. "To be on the safe side, we did *two* proposals. Just in case." He reached into the truck and pulled out a leather folder, extracted a sheet of paper and handed it to me.

Their proposal was very thorough. I'd looked at a lot of these in my career, and often my clients would howl in despair because although I'd explained it to them, they really didn't understand the term *estimate*, and would invariably complain about every dollar spent over what they'd signed on for. The bottom number here looked substantial, but I could see that they had covered pretty much everything, down to the cost of kitchen hardware and sod for the front lawn.

I'd bought the house, cash, from the money I'd received from my mother's insurance. I'd taken out a construction loan, using her house as collateral, knowing I'd be able to pay it off when it sold. So the actual cost of the work didn't scare me, and seemed very much in line with what I'd seen from other contractors over the years.

I handed the paper back to Mike. "Where do I sign?"

Steve, who I already dubbed the silent brother, spoke up. "We'll draw up an official contract after you get these plans approved." Ah, so he was also the *business* brother. Mike's role was obviously sales and schmoozing.

I nodded. "I'll go to the zoning office first thing Monday. And where can I find you later Monday afternoon?"

Mike pointed across the street. "Right there."

"Really? You're building the retail space?" I asked.

Mike nodded. "Yep. Our first venture into commercial development, and I think we picked a winning project. Small, classy, and the guy who's behind the project is just great. Now, Terri mentioned that you're from Rehoboth, so you might have heard of him? Daniel Russo?"

And that's when my heart dropped down into the pit of my stomach.

I looked over at Terri, whose eyes got big and wide. She swore, very softly, but just loud enough for Steve to hear.

"What?" he asked.

Terri pointed at me. "Her ex."

Mike's eyes were wide. "Ex what? Husband, business associate, partner in crime?"

I cleared my throat. "Ex-person-I-lived-with. Whom I haven't seen or spoken to in over a year."

"Well, you'll be seeing a lot of him now. He's down here, checking up, about once a week. In fact, I think he's going to be renting a place right here in town, so he can spend even more time. But—" Mike was grinning now. "This street gets busier as the season wears on. Heck, maybe if the traffic is bad enough, you won't see him at all."

I took a deep breath and held it. Daniel.

Daniel Russo had been, until just over a year ago, the man in my life, my friend, roommate and lover. After I left him, I realized that my love for him was not a grand passion, but rather a comfort, a safe place to be that fit in with the rest of my safe life. As my mother's illness worsened, I moved back in with her. I knew that risk—breaking with Daniel might very well mean living the rest of my life alone. At my age, how great were the chances of finding love again? But if I was going to start taking chances, here was the place to start. So I moved from his house back to my mothers' and never looked back.

Daniel had not wanted me to leave. At all. In fact, he more than once offered to let Mom move in with us, so I could care for her there. But Mom had wanted to die in her own house, so I packed up my clothes and books and went back to the house I'd grown up in. After Mom died, he called, then called again. I never picked up, and he finally stopped. And now he was going to be working on a project directly across the street from my new home.

I couldn't begin to imagine what it would feel like to see him again. What would I feel? Regret? Guilt? Would I be tempted with the idea of returning to a relationship that, if nothing else, had made me feel secure? All I could do was wait and see.

I stuck out my hand. "Gentlemen, I'll talk on Monday. It's been a pleasure."

Steve shook my hand and went over to get in to the driver's side of the truck. Mike also shook my hand, but held it, and I felt a jolt that went right up my arm, bounced around my chest, then headed due south.

"Just remember," he said. "The universe has a way of telling you things."

"Oh? And what is the universe trying to tell me right now? That I should have put a bid on a spanking new condo instead of this place?"

He shook his head and dropped my hand, but I could still feel the tingle. "No. I think buying this little bit of scruff here will be good for you. You look like a woman willing to take a chance."

I stared at him. "I've spent an awful lot of my life trying to play it safe."

"And it brought you right here, where you don't have much of a choice. See? It *is* telling you something."

I felt a smile. "Yes. It's telling me I've got a smooth-talking contractor who likes a little drama at the expense of others along with his morning coffee."

He threw back his head and laughed. "Exactly." He leaned forward. "We got your back on this thing. Don't worry." Then he got back in the truck.

I watched them drive away with so many emotions going through my head I didn't even know where to start sorting them out.

"Maybe he's right," Terri said. "Maybe the universe is telling you that Daniel is the one for you after all."

I scowled at her. "Terri, you never liked him."

She shook her head. "No, not exactly. I just never thought he was good enough for you. And he never asked you to marry him."

"Because I made it clear I didn't want to marry *him*. Listen, Terri, Daniel and I were together, but the last few years had been...tepid. I mean, we were more like friends with limited benefits. If I really loved him all that much, don't you think I would have tried a little harder for us to stay together?"

Still...would it be awkward? Embarrassing? After all, I'd very easily put him out of my mind, and now he'd be working across the street. I walked back to my slightly tilted porch, sat on the bottom step and buried my face in my hands. "Crap."

Terri sat beside me and put an arm around my shoulders. "Not to worry, Chris. I'm here for you. Besides, you'll be busy with this house."

I looked back at the open front door. "Yes. This house. Terri, if I've learned only one important lesson from this, it's to always take my own advice."

"And what advice was that?"

"To never buy anything without looking over the house inspection report with a fine-tooth comb."

"I did look it over."

"But *I* never saw it. And when you told me that there weren't any big issues..."

"Well, inspection found that the foundation was solid, no termite damage, no water damage and structurally the house was sound. The inspector didn't say anything about the mechanicals or interior because, well, there *were* no mechanicals or interiors for him to inspect in the first place."

She was right. Her reasoning made perfect sense. It was all my fault. If I had just asked her to send it to me anyway...

If I had fully realized the extent of the work needed, would I have said no? If I had pulled out of the deal, I probably *would* have found a nice, brand new condo somewhere close. And then what?

Here I had a chance to build my own place from, literally, the ground up. Something that, in the back far corners of my mind, I had always wanted to do.

And I would have a chance to see Daniel again. Did I still love him? Always. But I knew that my love for him had changed.

And then there was Mike McCann, with those twinkling blue eyes and that slightly crooked, slightly wicked grin.

Steve McCann was obviously a very attractive man, but all for the rest of that day, and the next, it was Mike McCann's handshake that I kept thinking about, and the tiny jolt of something I'd felt that I hadn't felt in a long time.

Garson Heller re-stamped my plans and reissued the permits without my having to sleep with him, although I might very well have offered. Then I walked to Susan Arnett's office, right over a jewelry shop on Main Street. She went over the blueprints, penciled in a few changes to the closets and praised the McCann brothers to the rooftops. She suggested I go across the Bay Bridge to Norfolk to look at flooring and kitchen appliances, but to choose my lighting from a few local people known for original and reasonable designs. She also gave me a list of antique and furniture consignment shops, as I told her I wanted a shabby, beach vibe. Then, she took my hand and squeezed it, welcoming me to Cape Edwards and telling me that everything was going to be fine. I believed her much more than I had Terri, because although she may have respected Steve McCann as a contractor, she showed no signs of wanting to jump his bones.

I walked back up the street and handed over the newly approved blueprints and all my new permits, as well as a sizable check to the McCann Brothers, LLC.

Terri, of course was working, so on Tuesday I shopped for appliances alone, picked out a bed and a couch to be delivered on demand, and since I was still obsessing about my floor, or lack thereof, wrote down the specs for my top three choices.

The entire back yard was cleared of saplings, weeds and debris to make room for the dumpster. I spent all day Wednesday watching as a truckload of lumber was delivered, along with shingles, Tyvek and all sorts of other things I didn't recognize at all except for the fact that they looked like they belonged on a construction site. I know that Mike had tried to find the owner of the empty lot next to me, with a mind to use the lot as a staging area, but hadn't any luck. So my little yard was crammed with material.

The work began.

And...it was pretty boring. Watching men tear old shingles off a roof gets old after about twelve minutes. Laying down plywood is also a bit dull, but at least there was, finally, a floor. And there were all sorts of strange smells that I didn't like at all.

I had bought a small lawnmower and cut the grass in the front yard the first night, after the crew left, so the next morning I could set up my beach chair and cooler, and from there I watched as the McCann crew swarmed like ants over the tiny house.

I also watched the progress across the street, which was way more interesting. The crew was bigger and there seemed to be a to more activity. I waved once at Mike, in a hard hat, and a few minutes later, he crossed the street, followed by a small and rather scruffy looking dog of questionable bloodline. Mike took off his hardhat and threw himself on the grass next to me.

"Don't suppose you have a beer in that cooler?"

I grinned. "Are you suggesting that you would drink on duty?"

"On duty? Hell, I'm barely workin' I like to think of my position as purely supervisory." The dog sat halfway between Mike and me, and looked alert, as if to spring at me if I made a wrong move in Mike's direction.

"That's Joe," Mike explained. "My roommate and emotional support animal."

I looked at him quizzically. "You don't strike me as the kind of guy who needs much additional emotional support."

"I don't, but if I call him that, he can come drinking with me. There's not a bartender around who'll turn away Joe."

"And is his position over there on the site also supervisory?"

"He does a heck of a lot more work than I do," Mike said, grinning.

I knew he was lying. I'd seen him at work, so I just waved him off. "What about my windows?" I asked.

He propped himself up on one elbow. "Susan Arnette, besides being a very nice person, is a contractor's dream. All standard sizes. You'll be sealed up tight by next week. I hate these rehabs where the owner wants some special order monstrosity that we have to wait six weeks for, and then we get an earful for not staying on schedule. This here house should be up by the end of the summer."

We watched as a man came over the peak of the roof from the back of the house and began to tear off a whole new row of shingles. "Have you been doing this a long time?" I asked.

"What? You didn't read the bios on the website?" He rolled his eyes. "We paid extra for that, you know. The McCann Story."

I laughed. "Sorry. I didn't even know you had a website."

"Welp, see, both Steve and I used to be financial bigwigs. I'm serious now. He has an MBA from Columbia, excusemeverymuch, and worked on Wall Street till the crash in '08. I was in Boston, also with an MBA, and we both got our butts kicked and lost our jobs and had to come running back here to lick our wounds."

He pulled on a blade of grass and stuck it between his teeth. I had already noted that his lips were full and looked rather soft. I found my eyes going back to his mouth every time that blade of grass moved. It was quite distracting

"Luckily," he continued, "we'd both worked construction before. That's what paid our college tuitions, so we looked around down here, saw all those broken-down summer cottages, and went into business for ourselves. And we've done pretty well for two hometown boys, I must say."

I stared, then let out a whoop of laughter. "So, that whole *gee, shucks* thing you got going on is, what? A show for your clients?"

He grinned. "Chris, I am a *gee, shucks* boy from way back. It's in my blood. You can take a man out of the Eastern Shore, but you can't scrape the Eastern Shore off the man, not even with putty knife."

"Hey."

I turned. Steve was standing on the porch, his hands on his hips. "What are you doing on my job site? Don't you have work of your own to do?"

"Joe and I are discussing important business here with our client," Mike yelled back. "And you are interrupting."

"And what is so important?"

"Windows. Go away, little brother. All your good looks are spilling out on this new-mown lawn."

Steve turned and went back inside.

"I guess that's my cue," Mike said, standing slowly and stretching his hands high over his head. "This front lawn doesn't look half bad now that's it's been cleaned up a bit. Who did you get to mow this, anyway?"

"I did it myself." I shaded my eyes with my hand as I looked up at him.

"'Though she be but little, she is fierce,'" he quoted.

"Trying to show off some of that MBA with a little Shakespeare?"

"I try to show off that MBA any way I can," he said. "It took me years to pay it off." He grinned. "I'd better get back to work before my brother comes on back here and starts hollerin'."

"Okay, then, but feel free to stop back any time," I told him. "And bring Joe. I like the strong, silent type."

"Why, thanks, I think I will. Will there be beer next time?"

"I'll make sure of it."

"You're already up for Favorite Client of the Year. A cold one or two will probably clinch it," he winked at me. "Next time, we'll talk a little more Shakespeare," he said, and went back across the street, Joe walking behind him without a backward glance.

I watched him as he walked away, and I had to admit the view was just fine.

When I made my second appearance at the Grove that Friday night, I was greeted like an old friend. I'd had several people stop by during the day on Friday to watch the activity at the house, and now they all had questions. I found myself drawing the floor plan on a napkin from memory. Luckily, Susan drifted by and flipped the napkin over, her lines straight and true and garnering murmurs of admiration.

"Susan is very good," Stella Blount whispered in my ear. "A little snooty, but she's original and talented." Stella, I knew, ran a shop on Main Street. She was a small, compact ball of energy with a splash of bright red dye brightening her Afro, and she radiated a solid earth-mother vibe. Karen was there again as well and invited me to try a yoga class. I declined without telling her that I pretty much despised exercise in general, yoga in particular. Karen introduced me to a tall, attractive bald man, who stuck out his hand to shake mine warmly.

"I'm Judd Mitchell. You must be Chris. I'd love to take some photos of the house as it goes from derelict to dream."

I smiled back at him. "That sounds like one of the HGTV shows Terri has been watching."

He laughed. "I don't do video, sorry, but it would make a great photo essay. I put some of my work online. Would you mind?"

I shook my head. "Not at all. In fact, it would be great to be able to look back and see how everything was done. How about Sunday?"

We agreed on a time, and he drifted off.

Marie Wu was also there. She was a real estate attorney, and although I knew her only slightly from previous trips to visit Terri, she sat beside me all through dinner and kept me laughing all night as we traded our strangest real estate stories. Then it was an early bedtime.

I'd spent most of last part of the week not thinking about Mike McCann. And by that I mean that I made a very concerted effort not to think about the way his gray hair curled, just a bit, at the base of his neck, and how his hands looks knotted and muscular and very capable. Then, I didn't think about what those hands might be doing if they were involved in something other than power tools and plywood and spray-foam insulation. What would they feel like, for instance, running through my hair, down the side of my arm, up the inside of my thigh...

Finally, Saturday afternoon, I knew I had to do something to pull my head out of the clouds, so I headed out to the Coop, one of my favorite places on the Eastern Shore. It was also where I had another good friend, albeit an odd one.

When I came down to visit Terri right after my divorce, almost fifteen years ago, I wandered into The Northampton Antique Co-Op, known as the Coop, a long, rambling building at the end of a rutted drive off the highway. Inside, the air was cool, and it had that musty kind of smell: old books and aged wood, dust and mold. There were at least thirty different vendors represented there, with stalls selling everything from vintage baseball cards to Victorian oak bedroom sets. Right away, I knew it was my kind of place.

I had bought a small framed print, and in paying by credit card, the woman behind the counter read my newly reacquired last name slowly, then looked up at me though eyes made bigger and blacker by layers of mascara.

"You're Italian?" she asked.

I nodded. My father had died when I was eight, and shortly afterwards my Irish mother moved from the busy Italian section in Baltimore to live closer to her brother in Rehoboth. I had fond memories of my paternal grandmother, widowed at sixty, who lived off of social security in a tiny walk-up apartment. Whenever we visited, there was a crowd of relatives: her cousins and their children, the neighbors down the hall, and aged old men from the neighborhood. There was always laughter and arguing, penny-ante card games and talk about the old days. And there was always a pot of what Nana called Sunday gravy on the stove, and a plate of delicacies from the Mastriano's Bakery on the kitchen table.

The woman behind the counter beamed. "I'm Celestina Montecorvo. Call me Celeste," she said. Then she turned her head and shouted into the back office. "Connie, come out here!"

An even older woman came out. The two women were immediately recognizable to me: short hair dyed pure black, thin, penciled-in brows, thick lashes and a red mouth.

"This is my sister, Constanzia. Connie. Do you live here on the Eastern Shore? We always like to make our Italian customers welcome."

I shook my head, smiling. "Sorry, just a visitor."

Connie grabbed my hand. "But you're staying a while? Maybe you could stop back and visit? Where are your people from?"

I had to think. "The Marches?" I said, dragging the name from a faint memory.

Celeste clasped both of her hands to her chest. "Us too! We might be family! Where?" She rattled off a series of place names that left me shaking my head and laughing.

"Sorry," I said. "I just don't know."

Celeste patted my hand. "Doesn't matter. Come back? We're closed on Mondays, but we live right in the back."

I had tried to back out gracefully, but they were so sweet and insistent that the following Monday I went back and sat in their tiny apartment behind the Coop, eating homemade sausages with broccoli rabe the likes of which I hadn't tasted since I was last in my Nana's kitchen. They represented something warm and familiar to me, and I went back to see them every subsequent trip. The last time I had been down, I had sat in their cramped kitchen and cried about my mother, then cried again when Connie said she was moving into a nursing home because of her most recent stroke.

As I walked in, I paused to let my eyes adjust from the bright sunlight outside to the considerably dimmer interior of Coop.

"Christiana, dear, it's so good to see you," Celeste called, coming out from behind the counter. She seemed even tinier than before, her back humped and misshapen under her flowered shirt. She reached up to kiss me on both cheeks.

"Is your dear mother gone?" she asked.

When I nodded, she embraced me again. "Oh, Christiana, I'm so sorry. But it's good you're here. The sea air will heal you."

I drank in the familiar smell of her: garlic and peppers, and a hint of mothballs. "How's Connie?"

Her face fell. "Not good. And that place..."She waved a hand and went back behind the counter. "I don't like that place. I want her somewhere else, but..." She rubbed her two fingers together against her thumb. "Who can pay?"

"Well, Celeste, I bought a house in Cape Edwards, so I'll be spending lots of money here."

Her eyes lit up. "Oh, how lovely! Would you come with me sometime to visit Connie? I know she would love it."

"Of course," I said. "Let me get a little settled first. And let me shop!"

She waved her hands and I felt a little tugging at my heart. She had aged so much since I'd seen her last, and she seemed so tired. Next time, I'd be the one cooking for her, I thought.

As soon as I had a kitchen.

Chapter Three

I had a budget. I didn't know what I was looking for exactly, but I knew how much I could spend. I spent almost an hour checking off the things I couldn't buy before starting my second loop, this time with a more determined eye.

I went back three times to an oak dresser, footed, with three drawers and an attached mirror. It spoke to me. It had a story, I could tell. And it was only two hundred bucks. I took a picture on my phone, and then another, then walked away to see it from a different angle.

"I've seen people spend less time looking at a car they were about to buy," Mike McCann said slowly. He'd come up behind me, and as I glanced up, he was shaking his head. "What, exactly, are you looking *for*?" He was dressed in a linen shirt and khaki shorts, his sunglasses pushed up to the top of his head. Joe was behind him, looking slightly bored.

I was totally surprised to see him. My heart rate jumped and I swear I got a little breathless. I was totally unprepared for such a reaction, and to hide my confusion I crouched down and held out a hand. Joe took a few tentative steps toward me, sniffed my open palm, and wagged his tail slowly.

"I'm impressed," Mike said. "He usually bites first and asks questions later."

I stood back up. "You're a liar, Mike McCann. I bet that dog is a complete marshmallow."

He grinned. "You're a pretty good judge of dogs."

"I've always wanted one, and if I could get one as well behaved as Joe, I'd jump right in." I turned back to the dresser. "I'm thinking this would be great in the bathroom. Instead of a regular vanity? What do you think?" I found myself smiling, and he smiled back.

"I think you don't even have *walls* in your bathroom. Aren't you rushing things just a bit?"

"Not at all. This is the very first house I've ever lived in that's going to be just mine, and if I see something I want, I'm going to get it. And I think this would be just fine, with a little cleaning, maybe scrape off this old paint?"

"You know, you could save me a whole lotta trouble if you just went to Home Depot."

"Yes, but look at this piece. It's the right height, the bottom two drawers could be used for storage, and that mirror..."

He raked his fingers through his beard. "Hmm." He got down on his knees and looked under the dresser, pulled out all the drawers and looked again, then stood with a sigh. "Yeah, this is pretty perfect. One of those square sinks on top, a few coats of poly...it'll work."

I beamed. "And look what else I found."

"Is it going to be more work for me?" he asked, his blue eyes twinkling.

"Probably. Or you could show me how to do it." I started down toward the next aisle. "Now, this armoire?"

"Is flying under a false flag. This is not an armoire at all. It's a tall kitchen cupboard."

"Whatever. But can it fit in where the hall closet is supposed to go? Look at all this storage! I can put some shelves in the top here, and these drawers are..." I pulled. The first drawer had opened quite easily, but the bottom was stuck.

"These drawers are painted shut," Mike pointed out.

"Not all of them. But what do you think? It's not too wide, is it?"

He shook his head. "No. Not too wide. And the height is about right, too. Okay, I'll give you this one. We can make the opening to fit this piece, if you want to take it on. You can strip the paint, do the sanding, hell, you can even change out the hardware." He was grinning now, and I could see the laughter in his eyes.

"You're mocking me, Mike McCann. Just you wait. I'm going to become a master at this stuff."

"Yes. Welp, let's see if you can get it all back to the house first." He glanced down at me. "There's more?"

I nodded. "Yes. But, you weren't here to help me with all this. I've got the rest. Really."

"The *rest*? God, woman, just how much were you thinking about buying?"

"Well, there's a set delivery charge no matter how many pieces I get, so I may as well just go for broke, right?"

He threw back his head and laughed. "May as well. Okay, what's next?"

"Are you sure? I mean, what did you come here for in the first place?"

He shrugged. "I collect old woodworking tools. Planes, saws, drill... any old piece of crap nobody else wants. Got a whole garage full. I have no idea what I'm gonna do with it all, but it just makes me feel good to know that if the apocalypse comes, and there's no more electricity in the world, I have the tools and can still build me a house. So, go on. What else you got?"

I jerked my head to the left. "I know we ordered a kitchen island from the cabinet place, but look at this, this long table. It's almost counter height, isn't it? And that shelf along the bottom is perfect for storing bowls and stuff." The table was long, over six feet, with a rough top and legs painted a dull red.

"Welp, we could sand down the top here, or maybe get you some nice butcher block. And you're right, it's a perfect height." Mike crouched down and looked at the underneath. "It's solid enough, for sure. And these red legs? Is that your *pop of color?*"

"You're mocking me again."

"Nope, not me. I'm just a small-town boy tryin' to get up to speed with your big-city design ideas."

I snorted. "You're not going to try to pull that *ah, shucks* BS on me again, are you? I've got you figured out, Mike McCann. I don't want my house to look like everyone else's," I said. "Besides, I like junk. And over there..." I raised my arms, hands together, both index fingers pointing.

He groaned and caught my hands, rocking them back and forth. "Woman, you're killing me here."

I almost jumped out of my skin. His hands on mine felt just right. I felt the heat of his palms, and electricity shot up both arms, across my chest, down my back and, well...down. He held them for just a second before dropping his arms and walking away, but in that second, I had lost my breath.

Maybe he was glib and dismissive, and maybe he was just humoring me because I was his client and paying him *lots* of money, but...

"Never mind. I think I'm done," I managed.

"Thank all that is holy. Okay, let's see Celeste and get this stuff tagged. You don't want anyone else grabbing up this treasure."

Celeste greeted Mike with a kiss on both cheeks, and carefully wrote down what I wanted, then graciously accepted my credit card. She handed it back to me with a smile. "Thank you, Christiana. I hope you enjoy all those lovely things."

Mike raised his eyebrows. "Christiana? That's not the name on that check you wrote us."

She beamed. "She's Italian, you know. That's her *real* name. Chris," she waved both hands in the air. "Chris is a man's name."

Mike looked skeptical. "Italian really? What with all those light-colored curls?"

"My mother was Irish," I explained.

"Ah," Celeste breathed. "Of course. You know, the Irish and the Italians, when they get together, they make very beautiful children."

Mike nodded slowly. "Yes, Celeste, they surely do," he said, his eyes never leaving my face.

I felt my cheeks start to burn and ducked my head. "Thanks, Celeste. We'll talk soon."

I went outside, thankful for the fresh air. Just when the rush I'd felt of Mike touching my hands had started to fade, he called me *beautiful?* What did that mean? I needed to put some distance between Mike and me and try to sort that out. I took a few deep breaths on my way to the car, and wouldn't you know, Mike was right behind me.

"We'll pick this up for you, Chris. I'll send somebody out here with a truck. That way, Celeste won't have to pay her driver, and we could save her a bit."

I looked back at the Coop. "Is the place in trouble?"

He shrugged. "Things will get better once the season starts, but she's worried about her sister, and I know that money is an issue for her."

Not only did he have sexy blue eyes and a killer smile, he was also a nice guy.

"You should buy the place, Mike. Just think of all that good rusty stuff in there."

He grinned. "What, and retire from that glamorous life of construction?" He chuckled. "No, not me. Even if I wanted to, I don't have any extra millions lying around."

I was shocked. "Millions? For that place? I mean, that building isn't in such good shape, and she doesn't even own the inventory..."

He shook his head. "Not the building. The twenty-some acres it sits on. Highway frontage. That's where the real value is."

He stuck his hands in his pockets. We were standing fairly close, and he seemed to be trying to decide something when Joe suddenly barked. We both looked. Joe had jumped into the open window of Mike's truck and was looking out the window.

"Well, I guess it's time to go," he said slowly. "See you Monday."

He walked to his truck, and I watched his truck turn up the drive, then got in my car and drove back. It wasn't until I was almost back to Cape Edwards that I realized I'd been grinning the whole drive home. Terri asked me, hours later, what on earth I was so happy about.

"Nothing," I said.

"Then why are you smiling?"

"I ran into Mike McCann at the Coop and he did something that made me...laugh," I said, trying to act like it didn't matter at all.

She raised an eyebrow. "Oh, Mike?"

I waved her off. "I know you want everyone to have a happily ever after, Terri, but he's not my type."

She believed me, even as I was having a hard time believing myself.

Judd, I found out, was in his late forties, gay, and had come to Cape Edwards on a photo assignment and never left. He and I spent about half an hour on Sunday morning walking through the bare bones on my house.

"Well," he said. "You've got the derelict part down pat."

I nodded. "You should have seen it before they cleared the back. And put up the new roof. And the floor. This is actually a few steps up." We finally sat on the porch steps and watched traffic stream by, toward the beach.

"You'll like it here," he told me. "The people are warm and friendly, and there's always something going on in town. And you can almost smell the bay."

I sighed happily. "I know. That's the best part, knowing I can walk down to the water any time I want."

He looked at me quizzically. "But...you're from Rehoboth?"

I laughed. "Yes, I know. But I was always working. I rarely got to the beach. Kinda stupid, isn't it? But here, I'll have the time."

"What are you going to do? Jobwise?"

I shrugged. "Don't know yet. I was in real estate."

He made a noise. "Forget that. You can't swing a cat around here without hitting six starving realtors."

"That's what I was afraid of. Maybe I'll wait tables at Sam's on Main." I wasn't all that worried about money right now. I'd be selling my share of my real estate business to my two partners, and we'd agreed on a five-year payment plan. I had scaled back on the day-to-day work of the business during the last months that mom was sick, and found, after going back, I really didn't enjoy it anymore. My two partners were more than willing to buy out my share. Between that and the rest of the money from Mom's house, I didn't really need a job. But what else was I going to do all day? And, eventually, I'd need to pump up my income if I wanted to do anything besides pay for the basics.

I heard some activity behind the house, and seconds later, Steve McCann came around and up the steps.

He shook hands with Judd. "I was driving by and saw you, so I thought I'd let you know that your kitchen cabinets have been ordered," he told me. "There's a six-week lead time, so the timing is perfect."

"Good to hear," I told him. I had spent half the day on Thursday agonizing over glazed versus unglazed cabinets before making the decision, and Steve had called and placed the actual order based on Susan's plans.

He looked at Judd. "You taking pictures?"

Judd nodded. "I'm thinking it would make a nice photo essay, the saving of a traditional bungalow. Most folks would just tear this down."

Steve grinned. "Well, if you want to photograph someplace that probably will be torn down, then you might want to head over to the Coop. Rumor has it, that's on the block and my favorite ex-sister-in-law has her eyes on it."

I sat up. Did he just say ex-sister-in-law? As in, Mike's *ex-wife*? And the Coop?

"I love that place," I blurted. "I've been there every time I've come down to visit. I was just there yesterday and bought a whole bunch of great stuff. Mike was there."

Steve made a noise. "Mike is always there. I sometimes think he buys all those tools of his just to throw Celeste some extra cash." He shook his head. "Mike loves that place, but then, he likes all sorts of cramped places full of rusty junk. But yeah, Amy may come back to town and sink her teeth into it, and I guarantee that she won't be as thoughtful a planner as Daniel Russo Associates."

Daniel had always been meticulous in his commercial spaces, doing everything he could to make sure the new blended in with the old. I had visited many of his projects and always marveled how aesthetically pleasing they ended up. Which was why, although I didn't relish a commercial property across the street from my house, I knew that at least it would be quite pleasant to look at. But maybe the ex-Mrs. Mike McCann...

"So, Mike's wife is in commercial development as well?"

Steve rolled his eyes. "Ex-wife, thank God. She's into commercial bulldozing, commercial don't-leave-a-tree-standing, and commercial big bucks. That's what she's into."

Well.

Steve waved a hand. "Later. Have fun taking pictures." He went around to the back of the house. I looked across the street to the quiet job site.

"I'd hate to see the Coop go," I muttered. "I love Celeste and Connie."

Judd shrugged. "It's outside the city limits here, so any zoning or planning goes through the county, and the county is more interested in tax revenue than whether or not a developer has the best interest of the community at heart. If the sale goes through, Amy McCann will be able to build whatever she wants there, and no one will stop her."

"She doesn't sound like a very nice person. How did she end up married to Mike?"

Judd chuckled. "That is an excellent question, one that we all asked at the time. She lives in Virginia Beach, and came across the Bay for some project or the other, met Mike, and in just a few months they were married. I think the phrase "whirlwind romance" is often used to describe the two of them. They lasted less than a year, then she filed for divorce and he, apparently, swore off women for the rest of his life. She still has business interests over here, and since they run in the same circles, it makes for awkward Chamber of Commerce dinners." He looked thoughtful. "The thing of it is, she *is* a nice person. I've met her, oh, maybe a dozen times over the years, and she's quite bright and articulate, has a wicked sense of humor, and genuinely enjoys talking to people. She's also a complete barracuda in her business practices, and people tend to remember only that side of her. Still, she and Mike were...an odd combination."

"Was she involved in the project across the street?"

He shook his head. "No. Although I believe she had put out feelers a year or so back. This company from Rehoboth did a real stealth job in getting that land. Amy was pretty upset that she lost out, I understand. And now Mike is doing the construction..." He grinned. "We're a pretty small town, but we are not without our intrigue."

We sat for a bit longer before he stood and stretched and then shook down the leg of his jeans. "I've got a shoot at noon. This was good. Good work. Let me know what the schedule is, and I'll try to stop by every few days, just to take a few shots."

I agreed and watched him walk down the sidewalk, back toward the beach.

I glanced at my watch. Terri had slept in, and we had a quiet day planned: lunch, the beach, and dinner and a movie over in Norfolk.

I locked up my little house and walked back to town. Mike had an ex-wife who apparently ruined him for other women. She'd been beaten out of a choice project by my ex-boyfriend. And she wanted to tear down one of my favorite shopping places in the world and possibly put up a tacky strip mall.

Suddenly, life in Cape Edwards had gotten a bit more interesting.

As I walked down to the house Monday morning, I decided that Mike McCann just might be worth not only a closer look, but a lot of other closer things. Now, maybe he was gun-shy around women, and maybe he wasn't, but there had absolutely been a moment there at the Coop, and I could play off that, be charming and sweet, maybe flirt just a bit...

Who was I kidding? I'd never flirted. I'd always been the one flirted *with*. By my high school boyfriend who became my ex-husband. By the much older Seth Somers, who had wanted a cute young lover to make *his* ex-wife jealous. And by Daniel, who couldn't understand why, upon our first meeting, I didn't think he was the most interesting man in the world. After trying for months to prove it to me, we finally agreed to live together and the rest, as they say, was history.

I'd never chased after anything I'd really wanted in my whole life, because I'd always been afraid of how badly I'd feel if I didn't get it. But I was in Cape Edwards now, and I'd already made a few steps in directions I never thought I'd go. And in my mind I had already christened this year as The Year of Taking Chances, so maybe, since I really wanted to get to know Mike better...

As I got closer to my house, my resolve got firmer, and by the time I reached the walkway, I was feeling like an Amazon: fearless, determined, and totally in control. I could do this. I could walk across the street, make charming small talk, bat my eyelashes...in fact, I turned and waited at the curb, then shot between the cars and rounded the corner of the job site.

And stopped dead.

Daniel Russo was staring at me, an understandably confused look on his face. He was dressed in a beautifully well-cut suit, his shirt gleaming white, tie perfectly knotted. He was standing next to Mike McCann, who was dressed in jeans and a rumpled button-down shirt, sleeves rolled up to the elbows, and scuffed workbooks.

"What on *earth*..." Daniel said.

Mike ran his hand through his beard. "That's right, you two know each other."

Daniel raised an eyebrow. "*Know* each other? Why, we..."

I gave myself an internal slap upside the head. In my mind, I imagined that, upon seeing him again, I'd be cool and completely in control. But my heart was doing funny little jumps and I felt a little out of breath, and as I tried to figure out what could be causing that kind of reaction, it occurred to me that maybe it had nothing to do with Daniel at all, and maybe, just maybe, everything to do with Mike.

I stepped closer, tugged on Daniel's very expensive lapel and reached up to kiss his cheek. "Daniel, how lovely to see you again. You can't even imagine my reaction when Mike told me that you were the developer here."

This was a rare treat for me, seeing Daniel actually surprised by something and at a loss for words. He glanced around. "Is there, do you suppose, anywhere we could go and *talk*?"

Mike was grinning. "Chris, why don't you take Daniel here across the street, show him your new place and, ah, bring him up to speed?"

Daniel's eyebrows shot up. "Your new place? Across the *street*? My God, Christiana, don't tell me *this* is where you're living now?"

He was the only person, besides my mother and Celeste to call me by my given name, and I felt a sad little turn in my heart. But of course, he had to be just a little bit of an asshole. What was so terrible about Cape Edwards? I narrowed my eyes at him.

"What's wrong with living here, Daniel? You make it sound like I just moved into the third circle of hell."

Daniel ran his fingers through his hair, which was rather long and marvelously thick, dark and shot with gray, with all sorts of curls that fell down around his forehead. He was not too tall, maybe 5'8", and slim, with a wide forehead and close-set eyes. He was not handsome, but attractive in a Lord Byron-ish sort of way, with a wild-haired bad boy kind of sexiness. Right now his brown eyes were wide, and I could practically see him backpedaling.

"Of course there's nothing wrong with *here*. After all, I'm here. It's just—" He looked at Mike. "Will you excuse me? Us? For just a few minutes?"

Mike nodded. "Of course. You two take all the time you need." He gave me a smile, and I saw that glint in his eyes again. Was he enjoying this little drama? Yes, of course he was.

Daniel and I crossed back to my side of the street, and as I started up the walk, I could hear him chuckling. "Of all the gin joints in all the towns, you have to be living across the street from mine?"

As it had countless times in the past, his humor put him back on my good side. I stopped, put my head down, and started to laugh. "I know. Can you believe this? Honest to God, Daniel, when Mike mentioned your name, I almost dropped over in a faint."

I turned to him. He was smiling at me, that dear, funny smile that had melted my heart so many times. It was good to see, and it was also good to realize that it didn't have the same effect. At all. "I'm happy to see you," I said. "And it's good to know you haven't changed one bit."

"And why should I change? I was practically perfect, you know. I've missed you," he said. "I mean, I *have* moved on, but...well, I always thought you and I had something rather special."

"We did have, Daniel. And I hope we can be friends."

He took a deep breath. "Well, as one friend to another, can I tell you that you have terrible taste in real estate? How on earth were you so successful at it for so long?"

"I know it looks rough, but you are a man of vision, Daniel. Don't look at what it is, but what it could be."

"It could be a major financial burden, that's what it could be."

"Don't be mean. Come on in. I can actually give you a tour because I have a floor now."

He put his arm through mine as we went up the walk. "Why are you making it sound as if having a floor is a big deal? Aren't you *supposed* to have one?"

"Yes." We went up the porch steps and into the house. "But it's a fairly new development." Inside, there were a few of the guys on tall ladders installing sheetrock to my very vaulted ceiling. There was also someone I didn't recognize, a big man with very dark skin sitting on the floor, his long legs stretched out in front of him. He was studying blueprints, and looked up as we walked in.

I looked around for Steve. Not visible. I looked down and cleared my throat. "Hi I'm Chris. I'm the owner. And you are?"

He got up. "I'm Alan Jones. I'm the electrician."

Daniel nodded. "Daniel. Just passing through."

I clapped my hands together. "Well, now that that ordeal is over, please tell me how easy this is going to be for you, Alan."

"Everything has to be replaced. You knew that?"

I nodded and listened, and mentally added up everything he was telling me and tried to remember what the McCann's estimate had listed for electrical. "Did Mike know this already?" I asked.

He nodded. "Yes. I had a quick look-see right after your friend? Terri? Anyway, right after she closed."

I felt a surge of relief. That meant the McCann's estimate was probably close.

"But you might want to think about a generator," Alan said. "During hurricane season, power goes out all the time. And maybe motion detector lights? You're right on Main Street here, and they'll be, ah, lots of foot traffic during the summer."

"I've already been warned about drunks wandering on my front yard. Let's go with some motion detectors."

Ka-ching.

"And your plans call for pot lights," he went on, "which means every time a bulb goes out, you'll need a very tall ladder. Might want to think about pendants."

Double ka-ching. "I just thought about them. An excellent idea. Is that all?"

Thankfully, he nodded, and Daniel stared at me. I caught his look. "What?"

"All this off-the-cuff decision-making. It's quite unlike you. Don't you want to run a spreadsheet and do a week's worth of comparisons?"

I shook my head. "Nope. Not anymore."

Daniel and I walked through the framed bedrooms, had a lively discussion as to where I was planning to my low-flow toilet, and then took a quick tour of my back yard. My PODS container had finally arrived, and it stood there close to the alley, along with three trucks, and two covered pallets of lumber. We finally ended up back on the sidewalk.

"Well?" I asked.

"I'm still trying to formulate my vision."

"Daniel, be nice. I needed a change. I needed a new start. And here, I know a few people, and there's the bay. Did you notice it? That big bluish thing off to the east?"

"Ah, yes. Chris Polittano and her love of all things beach related. You're even closer here than in Rehoboth. And I must say, the proximity to town is ideal. And when I'm done here, you can walk across the street for banking and bagels."

I looked across the street. "Isn't this a bit small time for you?"

He nodded. "Yes, but this area is going to explode in the next few years, and I wanted a foot in the door."

"You're not going to buy up everything and ruin my neighborhood, are you?" Daniel, once he found a location to his liking, tended to look for ways to sprawl.

He laughed. "No. I don't think so. I try very hard to not ruffle the locals. Although I'd love a larger project. You know, for years I've been trying to find a juicy mixed-use project, like a mini-village, with shops and cafes and things all at street level and lofts and studios above."

"That sounds great, Daniel, but not in Cape Edwards, okay?"

"Deal. But it seems that I'm not the only player in this game. Is Mike married?"

I looked at him. "Divorced. Why?"

"Well, according to one of my more recently acquired sources, there's an Amy McCann that's about to make a very big play for a large parcel of land just north of here. If she gets it, the landscape could really change."

He must have been referring to the Coop. I wanted to question him further, but his cell phone rang.

He glanced at it. "I really need to take this," he muttered. He gave me a quick peck on the cheek. "Later, neighbor," and walked away, across the street, cell phone to his ear.

I went back to my lawn chair until lunchtime, waiting to see if Mike would appear. He didn't, and I went home and ate two pints of ice cream for lunch.

Tuesday morning I met my neighbor.

I'd been curious about who lived in the tiny house next door, with a perfectly green lawn and carefully tended rose bushes. Tuesday morning, she was waiting for me at the end of my sidewalk, a small, gray-haired woman with very black skin and and eyes that glittered behind pink-framed glasses.

She held out her hand. "I'm Ava Wilson. Most folks call me Miss Ava. Sorry it's taken me so long to meet you, but I've been tending a sick grandchild. Welcome to Cape Edwards."

Her voice was clipped and precise, not at all the relaxed drawl I'd been hearing. I shook her hand, which was dry and firm and surprisingly strong for such a small woman. "Thank you. I'm Chris Polittano. You're not from around here either, are you?"

She smiled, showing teeth too perfect to be natural. She was dressed in a simple housedress of pale blue cotton and wore comfortable-looking shoes. "No. From Detroit. I've spent over thirty summers here and I never did pick up that accent." She shook her head. "Not that I'd want to. Sometimes, I can hardly understand what these folks are saying. I'm living here year round now, so maybe I'll finally start sounding like a native, but I doubt it." She nodded toward the house. "I'm so glad you're fixing the place up. It was quite lovely years ago. And an empty house is a bad neighbor." She turned her head to look across the street. "I would have preferred that place stay empty, but more business will be good for the town. We need the dollars for our schools and roads, and I've been told it's going to be quite nice when it's all finished."

I smiled. "Yes. I've heard that too. I wonder, do you know who owns the lot on the other side of me? We're trying to get permission to put some lumber and pallets of construction material on there. My back yard is tiny.

She shook her head. "I've never known who owned that, but you probably shouldn't disturb anything over there. A Delmarva fox squirrel has made a nest in one of those trees, and I'm just hoping she stays."

"Aren't squirrels kind of commonplace around here?" I asked.

She shook her head. "Not that squirrel. She's special. I call her Bella. But please, don't try to feed her." She clasped her hands together and smiled gain. "Well, it was lovely meeting you. I'm not around much. I volunteer at the Nature Center and spend a lot of time with my church. But if you see me home, please come right up on the porch and we'll have some tea. I'm not antisocial, I just forget myself sometimes. I'll be eighty, and I can pretty much only think about one thing at a time."

I watched as she walked back around to her front gate and shut it behind her. She walked pretty quickly for someone going to be eighty.

I looked over to the vacant lot in interest, expecting to see a flamboyant squirrel make an appearance, perhaps with a startling white stripe down it's back. But the trees were silent. I set up my lawn chair, and I kept looking over to try to catch sight of my treasure of a squirrel, but no luck. The ones I did see looked pretty commonplace to me.

Terri sent me a text on Wednesday telling me not to make any plans for the night, because it was Karen's birthday, and all of her friends were going out to celebrate. I sighed as I read it. She and her friends were the only people in town I'd be making any plans *with*. Did she think I had a secret life somewhere, and that I'd be running off with anyone else?

I'd been to the pier before. We usually drove there in Terri's golf cart, which she'd been parking next to my car in her neighbor's grassy yard. I took a quick shower when I got home, as did Terri, got the golf cart, picked up the birthday girl, Karen from her studio, and buzzed our way to the pier. It was barely a mile, so we were there plenty early, grabbed a long table, and bought beer and crabs. Karen was turning fifty-one. Her gray hair and wrinkled forehead had made me guess older. When I whispered my surprise to Terri, she nodded.

"She's into an all-natural lifestyle, which eliminates hair dye, wrinkle cream, and encourages long walks in the sun with minimal sunscreen." Karen's body, however, perfectly reflected that healthy life-style: she was toned and fit and looked amazing in everything I'd seen her wear. I felt a bit envious as I watched her devour cracked crab, corn on the cob, and a seemingly endless supply of biscuits. Maybe there was something to all that yoga after all?

Karen put down her corn and jumped up, waving.

"Here we are!" She called. I looked up and saw a couple coming toward us. The man looked familiar, as did the woman. Was that Jenna?

"She looks stunning," I whispered to Terri, who nodded, her eyes wide. Jenna wore a dark green slip dress that floated over her slender body. Her hair was down and fell in soft curls down her back, and her eyes sparkled.

"Craig, wow, hi! Thanks for coming!" Karen hugged Jenna, then Craig "What's the deal?" She teased him. "I never see you outside of Sam's."

"Special occasion," he said. "It's not every day you have a birthday. How could I resist?"

Karen looked surprised at his response, but before I could poke Terri for an explanation, he waved at us from across the table.

"Ladies. How's the house coming along?"

I shook my head. "I hate the smells. Everything smells. Fresh-cut lumber, drywall goop, heavy-duty wood glue, that stuff they use when they're soldering pipes...this experience has introduced me to an entirely new range of bad smells that I never knew existed."

Terri leaned toward Craig. "I love the smell of fresh-cut lumber."

He grinned. "Me too. What are you eating? It looks delicious."

Karen motioned with her hands. "No table service here. Just go up to the counter and order."

Craig turned to Jenna. "Come with? I have a feeling I'm going to need a pro."

I watched as they went up to the counter. "What gives?" I asked Terri.

She shrugged. "I haven't a clue. That's the most I've heard him say at one time since he got here. He was practically charming."

Karen leaned over Terri to whisper. "And you cannot tell me that Jenna looks that good just because she likes the band."

I looked round. I'd noticed the stage, and now saw people fiddling with the equipment. "Music?"

Terri nodded. "Oh, yeah. Michigan Zydeco. They are *so* good. I tried to invite Steve out here tonight, but he said he was working. What's going on over there that he's staying this late?"

I shrugged. The crew left at six every day that I had stayed that late, and Steve had gone with the rest of them. "He's not working at my house," I told her.

Across from us, at the end of the table, sat Stella Blount with a striking woman with hair in dreadlocks, wearing a bright coral shift that glowed against her black skin. I waved at Stella, and she grinned.

Jenna and Craig came back, and Jenna went over to talk to Stella as Craig sat back on his stool, his eyes following Jenna.

"How are your girls liking summer here on the peninsula?" Terri asked him.

His face lit up. "They're having a great time. That recreational program they have here for the kids is a lifesaver. And Jenna is great, just great with them. I don't know what I'd do without her."

He glanced at me and smiled, but I suddenly knew that Terri had been right about him. This man was definitely taken.

I nudged Karen. "Do you know the Coop?"

She frowned. "That old place up of Rt. 31? What about it?"

"Do you know if it's for sale?"

She shook her head.

I looked at Terri, who shrugged. "That piece of gossip has not made it to the post office. What's going on?"

"Nothing, but Mike McCann's ex-wife may be buying it." I tried to keep my voice casual. "Do you know her?"

Terri shook her head. "Not at all. But I do know her reputation. She's very successful and depending on who you talk to, she's successful because she's a brilliant businesswoman, or because she's a wicked viper who goes after her competitors with a machete and no conscience."

Karen snorted. "Men will always say that about a successful woman.'

Craig shook his head, laughing. "Not all men. I, for instance, have only the utmost respect and appreciation for most of the working women I know. Jenna is competent to the extreme, Stella is a brilliant salesperson, and Glory Rambeau could, without a doubt, run this whole country with one hand tied behind her back."

"Who's Glory?" I asked.

Terri grinned. "The chef at Sam's on Main, and Craig here is right about her. And I hear nothing but good things about Dr. French down there," she said, nodding to the other end of the table. "But when it comes to Amy..."

"Commercial real estate is tough," I said. "I know that Daniel had to work his ass off. He's the one that mentioned Amy was going after something big, and I was just curious. I love the Coop."

Terri leaned in. "Chris here was practically adopted by those two old ladies."

Karen raised an eyebrow. "Connie and Celeste?"

I shrugged. "It's an Italian thing. They fed me and we bonded for life. They're just so sweet, and Connie is in a nursing home now and I guess they really need the money."

Craig had been playing with his empty cup when a curvy blond, who looked older after a second look, grabbed his hand and pulled him on the dance floor. Craig may have been taken, but apparently no everyone had gotten the memo.

Terri nudged me as I watched him go up to the dance floor. "Ask Marie about the Coop," she said in my ear. "She hears all sorts of things."

I nodded, got up and moved to the other end of the table.

Marie Wu was sitting with Stella Blount and Dara French. I crouched down beside her and tried to talk above the music.

"Have you heard anything about a sale of the Coop?" I asked her.

She frowned, then shook her head. "I know Celeste is probably hurting for money, but..." She pulled out her phone and hit a few keys. "I just gave myself a reminder. I'll check with a friend of mine in the county office and see if there's been any activity around the place. Usually, if someone is interested in a piece of property that's not on the market, they check tax records, liens, that sort of stuff."

I smiled and tried to talk over the music. "Thanks."

I went back to my seat and watched the dancers. At one point, Craig and Jenna were dancing together, a sweet, slow dance, and there was no chance of even a sliver of moonlight slipping between them. How nice, I thought. They fit together so nice. I wished I had someone who I fit together that well with. I suddenly pictured Mike McCann and me, standing in the moonlight, arms around each other, our lips almost touching...

I took a gulp of cold water. The picture was still there. Maybe if I dumped the whole thing, ice and all, over my head?

I had a feeling it was going to take more than that to get Mike out of my head.

Chapter Four

The next morning on my way down to the house, I saw Jenna come flying out of Sam's on Main. She knocked over a woman and her kids, sending beach toys across the sidewalk. She fumbled to pick them up and I hung back. She was obviously upset, and I didn't feel like I knew her well enough to try to intervene. I hurried down the sidewalk as she crossed the street at a run and got into her Jeep.

Maybe I'd been wrong about the night before. Maybe she and Craig didn't fit so well together after all.

I was a fun night, and I was careful to drink lots of water instead of beer, and completely stayed away from the tequila. I had given myself a bit of a pep talk at one point while in the ladies room, then made myself go on to the dance floor. Its not that I didn't like to dance, I'd just always been afraid I'd make a fool of myself. But I told myself it was all part of my new take-a-chance outlook, and I'd had fun. I'd even learned to flatfoot, which didn't require too much effort, just coordination.

As I walked down to the house, I thought again about some kind of job. What, exactly, was I going to do with myself once the house was finished? I'd gotten my first job at sixteen and had been working ever since. I waited tables on the weekends during college, spent the summers back in Rehoboth as a lifeguard, and worked a few boring but educational office jobs before settling into real estate. Setting up another real estate office here looked like it would be difficult with all the competition. I hated the nine-to-five office drill. I wondered what the demand was for a fifty-year-old lifeguard.

When I got to the house, the front porch was missing. Not the whole thing, but the steps, the floorboards and all the columns had been replaced by four-by-fours.

I went through the empty lot around to the side of the house, looking, as I usually did, for the super-squirrel, Bella. This time, I saw her. She was larger than the other gray squirrels, and much lighter, her tail as long as her body. She was in the weeds and looked up at me. I swear she winked before scurrying up the trunk of a pine tree.

I saw the new side door had been roughed in, with a makeshift ramp going up. I gingerly stepped up and went in.

Through the forest of beams and uprights, I could see Steve and a half-dozen men crowded in a corner where I knew my kitchen was going to be. Now that there was a floor, I quietly made my way over.

I cleared my throat. "Hey, guys. I thought today I'd start helping out a bit. You know...a little nailing, a bit of carrying stuff around, just helping."

Tyler, Steve's foreman, made a very rude noise, then stopped abruptly as Steve shot him a look.

"Well, ma'am we could sure use the help." Tyler said. He was young. In fact, he was about fourteen in my mind, but I knew that couldn't be his real age.

Steve's mouth twitched. "We're still at a stage where there's a lot of heavy lifting. But these boys have it all under control. How about a road trip? Have you picked out your countertop yet?"

I shook my head. I had looked forward to doing some actual work, but given the option of shopping... "Nope. But don't we need to match it to the cabinets?"

Steve nodded and took me by the arm, leading me away from his crew. "I have a cabinet sample. They sent it over as soon as the order was placed, so we can take it with us."

I twisted around to try to get one last look at the crew. "Are you sure I can't help?"

We went down the ramp and he opened the passenger-side door of his truck. "We're good. Hop in."

We went north, and after the first three minutes, Steve started talking. A lot. He talked about what was going on with the house, a problem with the porch foundation, what was going on across the street. He was a good storyteller, I'll give him that, but it was very much a monologue. I managed to get in a few questions, but that was it.

Picking out a countertop was just as excruciating as picking out the cabinets, and when the salesperson then directed us to the back-splash, I almost burst into tears. Steve smoothly took control pulled out three options, briefly gave me the pros and cons of each, and five minutes later, we were done. I deliberately chose something a little bit different from the other samples, a quirky hexagonal tile with a bit of metallic shimmer. I was still making the conscious effort to step out of my comfort zone, and I found this decision didn't leave me feeling a though I'd made some dreadful mistake. I was getting better at this, I thought as we drove back down to Cape Edwards.

"How about lunch?" Steve suddenly suggested. It was barely noon, but I nodded. "Sure. That would be nice."

We drove past Cape Edwards to the very tip of the peninsula, and he turned the truck in to a tiny place, right on the water. It looked like the kind of place local talent met to discuss the best place to bury a body.

"It's not crowded," I said. The tourists were probably afraid to enter.

Steve held open the door. "Never is. It's a local place."

I walked into a blast of freezing air. It was a simple setup: a long bar and a dozen tables by the window. Outside, I could see a deck and more tables.

"Drink?" Steve asked.

"No, thanks. Just water."

Steve nodded at the bartender. "Water and a Bud." He reached across the bar and grabbed a few laminated menus, then motioned for me to go outside.

The sun was hot, so we settled under a faded umbrella. The menus leaned heavily toward fried fish. A young kid, probably barely old enough to be serving beer, brought our drinks.

"Steve," he muttered in greeting.

"Hey Chuck," Steve said back. "I'll have the platter. Blue cheese. Tartar." He handed the menu to the kid, who didn't write anything down, just looked at me.

"Ah," I scanned the menu again. Was everything fried? "Crab cake sandwich, please."

He took my menu. "Salad?"

"Ah, sure."

Pause. "Dressing?"

"Oh. French."

Another pause. "Tartar sauce or cocktail?"

"Tarter. Thanks." Anything else I was supposed to automatically know?

Chuck moved away.

"So, I guess you're a regular?" I asked Steve.

He nodded and took a long pull on his bottle of beer. Apparently, mugs were not an option. "Yeah. Been coming here since I was a kid." He pushed his sunglasses to the top of his head and stared at me for a moment. "I kinda monopolized the conversation on the way down here,'" he said. "Sorry about that. I like to talk about my work."

I shrugged. "That's okay. It was interesting."

"Probably not as interesting as you. Tell me something about yourself. Something you don't tell other people."

I sat back, a little surprised at his interest. "Well, I have a degree in art history, and I wanted to be a museum curator."

He chuckled. "Well, those jobs are hard to come by. Terri said you were in real estate. That's a leap."

I shrugged. "I had to do something. I also like architecture, and real estate gave me a chance to go snooping into people's houses."

He grinned. "Now, that's honest."

I laughed. "Yes, well, honest is something I try to be."

The salads arrived. There was a mixture of greens, thinly sliced cucumber, radishes, red onions and a wedge of ripe, red tomato. The dressing, served on the side, was so thick I had to spread it on the salad with my fork. It was delicious.

"How is it that the tourists don't come here?" I asked after scraping my salad plate clean.

"We don't tell them about it," Steve said. "There are a few places around here that we keep to ourselves. Have you been to DeeDee and Jacks yet?"

I had, actually, every time I'd come down to visit. It was a favorite of Terri's, the perfect dive bar, but with excellent food.

"Buck A Beer Tuesdays," I said. "I love that place."

"We'll have to go," he said. "Maybe next week?"

I froze, my water glass halfway to my mouth. What was that? Being social? A date? I'd been out of the dating scene for over twelve years, and knew I wouldn't recognize the landscape, even with a map and seasoned guide. "Terri and I go there all the time," I managed. "We'll probably see you there."

He shook his head. "What is it with you women, anyway? Always in packs. I've noticed that a lot more in the past few years. It's a lot harder to approach a woman when she's surrounded by other women."

I pointed my index finger at him. "That's the point."

A plate was dropped in front of me. "More beer?" the kid asked Steve.

Steve nodded, and as Chuck moved away, Steve's hand shot out to grab his arm.

"Hey, Chuck, be polite. Ask the lady here if she wants anything else."

Chuck glared, then turned to me and mumbled.

"More water. Please."

He mumbled, again and moved on.

I took a bite of sandwich. The crab cake had the perfect ratio of crabmeat to filling, and it was absolutely delicious. After three of four hurried mouthfuls, I swallowed, drank some more water and said, "So, I guess the great food makes up for the crappy service?"

Steve waited until he finished chewing. "An even trade-off, right?"

I couldn't answer, because my cheeks were stuffed, so I just nodded.

He grabbed the check when it came. "Business expense," he said, laughing, but I bet he meant it.

The trip back to Cape Edwards wasn't as chatty, but we talked and even laughed. He seemed a nice man. His good looks were a distraction, and I knew those beautiful eyes and devastating smile made him seem more interesting than he really was, but I enjoyed his company. I could certainly see why Terri was so hot for him. I asked him to drop me on Main Street because I wanted to go up to Terri's condo and change. He pulled the truck up in front of her place, blocking traffic, as I fumbled for my purse.

"Well, thanks again for lunch. I'll be at the house in a bit."

He nodded, half smiling. "Yeah. That was fun. So what about DeeDee's and Jacks? Maybe without your entourage?"

I think my jaw hit my chest before I could even think. That was absolutely a date.

"Ah, gee, Steve, thanks. Really. But I'm kind of, you know, feeling my way around, and I think I'm going to just stay with my, ah, entourage for now."

He looked at me steadily. "Listen. You'll probably hear things about me. How I change women like most men change socks. But there are two sides to every story. And the women around here, well, they expect certain things from me. That doesn't mean that's how *I* want things to be. But, that's how things are. Remember that."

I gulped, thanked him for lunch, and jumped out of the car, sprinting across traffic and causing several horns to blow.

Oh, my God. *Now* what was I supposed to do?

I needed advice. Steve McCann, the object of my good friend Terri's desire, had apparently asked me out on a date. I needed someone wise. Someone who knew the local landscape. And would pull no punches.

I hit the street and started walking.

Stella Blount's shop, Tidal Gifts was crowded, and as I entered, it didn't look like she was going to get any kind of a break any time soon, making it the wrong place to be. I smiled and waved, and headed back out the door.

I started walking down Main Street, realized I was heading right for my house, so I turned down and walked to Edwards Boulevard, the residential street that ran parallel to Main. I always liked this street. The Cape Edwards elite had built their homes there years ago, and the graceful brick Victorians still stood. As I walked by one house, under obvious renovation, I saw the McCann construction sign on the lawn and froze. This must have been Dara French's house. Was I going to be walking right past Steve McCann after all? I ducked my head and hurried past.

Getting lost in Cape Edwards was impossible, so when I ran out of Boulevard, I simply turned right to head back to Main. As I passed a small, fanciful brick building with a simple sign in the window. Yoga. Karen's studio.

It must have been a gas station in a former life, because the main building had arched windows and an improbable round, peaked roof, and there was a space to the side that had once been a garage. Where the bay doors had been were now tall frosted windows. I went up to the door and went in.

Sure enough, there was a small desk and a few comfortable chairs in the entry, and a blue doorway. There was a large, airy studio off to the side. There was classical music playing, but the rooms were empty.

"Hello?" My voice echoed, and after a few seconds, footsteps came from behind the blue door.

"Chris? Hi! Come to check out the place?"

Karen looked trim and toned in a simple black sleeveless tank top, leggings, and a colorful skirt tied across her hips. Her gray hair was on top of her head, and her face glowed.

"Ah, maybe. I mean yes. Crap. Karen, Steve McCann just took me to lunch."

She folded her arms across her chest. "Oh?"

"Terri has a thing for him. Did you know that?"

She nodded. "Yes. Did *you*?"

I threw myself into a chair. "My day started out with me walking down to the house. I was actually going to try to do some work. They all laughed at me."

"All?"

"Well, no. Steve was very polite. He suggested we pick out a countertop and backsplash instead. I said yes. You know that scene in *Moscow on the Hudson*? Where Robin Williams turns down the coffee aisle and has a breakdown because of all the choices? Well, that was me trying to decide between granite and quartz. This rehab stuff in not for the faint of heart."

She sat next to me. "And?"

"And on the way back, he suggested lunch."

She nodded. "That's reasonable. How was it?"

"I don't know where we ate, but it looked like a dive and the food was terrific. And he's a nice man. Interesting to talk to and an absolute joy to look at."

She lifted her eyebrows, which were unplucked and looked to be rather woolly. "Yes, that he is. None of us really know him, except Jenna. She went to school with him. She was a few years behind him, but she's always said he was a jock and a skirt chaser."

"He asked me out to DeeDee and Jacks. I wasn't sure if he meant it as a date or not."

"If it didn't just come up in casual conversation," she said dryly, "he probably meant it as a date."

"Yeah. I kind of changed the subject, and then as he was dropping me off he asked again and I kind of had to brush him off. But the intent was pretty clear."

"Oh. Oh, dear."

"And then he said that I shouldn't pay attention to all the talk about how he chases women around, because, as he rightfully pointed out, there are two sides to every story."

We sat there for a few minutes.

"Karen what am I going to do? What can I tell Terri?"

She sighed. "I don't know. She seems to think they made some sort of connection."

"Possibly. Then why would he ask me? He doesn't even *know* me."

She shrugged. "Maybe that's why. You're fresh meat."

I gave her the side-eye. "I'm not supposed to be listening to that sort of talk, remember?"

She sighed. "He does have a reputation of sleeping with pretty much any woman who asks."

"Does he get asked a lot?"

"Apparently, yes. His, ah, prowess has been discussed in some of the finest women's restrooms in town."

"Then...I mean, he's not out there seducing virgins. All he's doing is saying yes."

She looked thoughtful. "That's true. I never looked at it like that, I guess."

"What about Mike? Does he have a reputation too?"

She chuckled. "Yes. For being the total opposite. Word on the street says he got burned so bad by his former wife, he doesn't even *look* at women."

I felt a wave of disappointment. Doesn't even look? How was I supposed to appear charming and sexy if he wasn't even going to *look?* "That's too bad. Mike is so funny and just, I don't know. He has this good-ole-boy persona going on, but he has an MBA. He was in *finance.* He's probably, like, brilliant. And I usually don't care much for beards, but his just... fits his face. I mean, I can't imagine him without it, can you? And those blue eyes..." I felt myself smile.

"Ah, Chris?"

I'd been off somewhere else, I don't know for how long, thinking about those blue eyes. I looked at Karen. "What?"

"You were talking about Mike?"

"Yes?"

"It sounds like he made quite an impression."

"What do you mean?"

"Did you hear what you were just saying?"

I looked down at my hands. "Wow."

"Uh-huh."

"I really did say all that, didn't I?"

"Yep."

"It almost sounds like I'm crushing, just a bit, on Mike McCann."

"Yep."

"And his brother has expressed, shall we say, an interest?"

"Yep." My shoulders slumped. "Crap."

She poked me in the side with her elbow. "Honey, if I were you, I'd stay the hell away from that house until you figure out what you're going to do about those McCann boys."

"I need to find a way to get Steve's mind off me and on Terri. That's the first thing."

She nodded. "That's a one course of action."

"Okay. So, how do I do that?"

"I have no idea."

I sighed. "If she knew he asked me out, she'd be upset. So you can't tell her."

"I wouldn't. Of course I wouldn't." Karen patted my hand. "You need to tell her."

"No, I don't."

"What if someone else does?"

"No one else *knows*. Except you." I stopped and gave her a long look. "Why do I feel like I'm in the ninth grade?"

She stood up and pulled her hair out of its knot and brushed her fingers through it. "Because when push comes to shove, all of life is like middle school." She bent forward, the top of her head almost touching the ground, and wound her hair back up again, securing it back in place with a thin covered elastic band. Then she straightened up. "How did you end it with Steve?"

"That I was still feeling my way around and was sticking to hanging with girlfriends."

She put her hands on her hips. The woman had wrinkles all over her face and well down her neck, but, gosh, her body was perfect. "And he took that well?"

"I have no idea. I wasn't sure he'd even asked me on a date, remember?"

She shook her head. "I know. It's a whole other realm of understanding, and I'm sorry I can be of no help. Unless you want to stay for my next class? You could probably use a bit of relaxation."

I pulled myself up off the chair. "No. With the way my luck is going, I'll pull six different muscles and end up flat on my back for a week. But thanks."

I let myself out and stood, feeling the sun beating down on my face.

She was right. I had to figure out what to do with those McCann boys.

I got a text from Marie Wu, asking me to meet her at Bogey's at seven.

I texted back yes and found her at the bar, sipping what looked to be a very cold martini. She was a striking woman, Asian, with sleek black hair and porcelain skin. She'd managed to save me a seat, and I slid in beside her.

"I've got all sorts of interesting news about Celeste and the Coop," she said.

I felt my jaw drop. "Already?"

She grinned. "There are certain advantages to small-town living." She took out her phone and hit the screen. "Amy Cortland McCann has made two inquiries, one last year and one this past March. Just looking at tax records. Celeste is paid up and there's no issue there, so Amy tried another route."

"What do you mean, route? You mean foreclosure? Surely the property is paid for?"

She nodded. "It is, and there are no liens. But she was looking for code violations, complaints, any summons issued by the building department...anything she would be able to use to apply pressure. Nothing's there. Celeste is a dear, but Connie is the brains behind the operation, and I'm pretty sure she wouldn't let anything slip." She sipped her drink. "I handled a case for them, oh, about eight years ago. Somebody had bought up the property behind theirs and was trying to get a right-of-way so it could be developed. It went nowhere." She sipped. "Then the sisters bought the property, because Celeste always wanted a pond, and I think there were ducks. Anyway I got to know them both, and Connie is an absolute shark about the business."

"So, Amy McCann is going to make a play anyway?"

She nodded. "Probably. I called around, and she's had at least two independent appraisals done. That bit of property is worth a fortune, but if Amy wants it, she'll have to pay full price."

"Do you know Amy?"

She made a face. "Anyone who has any dealings with real estate in this part of the state knows Amy. She's tough as nails and has made some brilliant moves in the past, but she's very much a slash-and-burn developer, so folks around here really don't like to sell to her. But if the money is right..." She arched her eyebrow. "What's your interest in all this?"

The bartender was hovering, so I ordered a glass of wine. "I like Celeste and Connie. I have gotten to know them over the years. I've eaten in their kitchen. I helped them weed their garden. They remind me of my grandmother, and when you're as short of actual family as I am..." I shrugged. "And they have cultivated this fantasy that we're from the same village in Italy, so we may as well be blood."

She sipped some more. "Well, my guess is they'll sell to Amy so that Connie can move from the state facility she's in now to a private nursing home. Connie's still sharp, it's just her body that's failed."

"So, they want this? I keep thinking that they're two poor old ladies getting forced out."

She made a noise. "No way. Nobody has ever forced those two to do anything. And I'm sure they'd rather have anyone else buy them out. Any other developer around here who's interested will probably back away when they find out Amy is involved. She fights hard. Usually she fights clean, but going against her can be unpleasant." She downed the rest of her drink in one quick gulp, closing her eyes and shuddered slightly. "Ah, that really gets the tension out." The bartender delivered my wine, and she ordered another.

"So no one would object if Amy put in a mall or outlet center?" I asked.

The bartender bought her drink and I watched as she sipped.

She shrugged. "It's a hard call around here. We really need the ratables. Our schools are old, the roads are crap...the county wants more taxable spaces, and Amy would probably provide that. Nobody wants to see all that beautiful green space get eaten up by concrete, but it's going to happen eventually." She sipped.

Something clicked in the back of my brain. "Is it zoned mixed use? I mean, what about condos or apartments?"

She looked thoughtful. "It can be rezoned easily enough, if the county sees a profit in it. Why? Do you know anyone with six or seven million dollars to spend?"

I drank some wine. "As a matter of fact, I do."

"It's too far from the water to be of any use as seasonal rentals."

"Sure, but how about basic loft and studio space? I don't know the market here at all. Would those sorts of units sell?"

She nodded. "Sure. Affordable housing, especially for the younger people, is really at a premium right now." She sipped some more. "Who are you thinking about? I can practically see the wheels turning."

I grinned. "Daniel Russo."

She raised an eyebrow. "Who?"

"Daniel Russo. Who's managing the retail project across the street from my house. We lived together for eleven years."

"Oh, that's awkward."

I shook my head. "No, not really. It was over a year ago, and I think we're both ready to be just friends."

"Good luck with that. I've never had that happen. In my life." She downed her drink, shuddered again, then flagged the bartender. "I have to go."

I drew back. "You're not driving, are you?"

She shook her head as she slid her credit card to the bartender. "God, no. After two of these, I can barely walk. Uber out front in ten minutes." She sighed and slid off her bar stool. "I hope you can get this Daniel Russo guy to throw his hat in the ring. And I hope he has the balls enough to go against Amy."

"He does. All I have to do is convince him."

She signed for our drinks with a flourish. "If he needs any help, wants any names, or needs a connection anywhere, have him call me. I'm no fan of Amy McCann, and seeing her go down would be better than two martini's on a hot, summer night."

I watched her walk out, and sat, finished my wine, and thought.

First, I had to talk to Celeste and ask her to hold off if Amy McCann approached her.

Then I had to talk Daniel into building his dream project here. Although I liked the idea of him staying on his side of the street, it made sense that he was the one to save Celeste's trees.

And *then* I had to find a way to either get Mike McCann out of my head or convince him that the two of us were a great match.

I mentally moved the Mike project up to position one, finished my wine, and walked back to Terri's.

Friday morning was rainy, as when I pulled up to the Coop, the parking lot was crowded with cars bearing out-of-state plates. Good for Celeste, I thought.

Then I went in and saw that although the place was crowded, there was no line at the counter of people buying. There was a pretty young girl sitting there, looking bored.

"Where's Celeste?" I asked.

She jerked her head toward the back. "She hasn't come over yet. Probably around noon."

"Is she okay?" I asked.

The girl shrugged. "Yeah. She's fine. She closed last night."

I nodded my thanks, walked out through the parking lot and around to the side of the building, where the entrance to the tiny apartment was hidden behind a huge rhododendron.

I knocked and heard a muffled, "Come in," and pushed open the door.

Celeste was sitting at her kitchen table, a tiny cup of espresso in front of her, reading the newspaper. She looked up. Her face was drawn and white, and she looked old and very tired, but she smiled broadly.

"Christiana, dear, what a surprise! Here, sit. Can I get you some espresso? Coffee?"

She started to get up, but I hurried over, gave her a quick kiss on the cheek, and patted her shoulder. "No, Celeste, please, don't bother."

She got up anyway. "It's no bother. Regular coffee, yes? And maybe some toast? I have jam from last year. Strawberry. Not my favorite, but Connie, she likes the strawberries." She was moving slowly between the giant gas stove and the refrigerator, her back hunched, her black hair obviously uncombed. "Is everything okay? Do you need something?"

"Yes, Celeste. I do. Can you please sit?"

But, of course, she couldn't, not until I had a cup of coffee in front of me and a thick slice of toast, slathered with strawberry jam.

She was finally back in her seat. "Now. What can I do for you?"

"You can put off Amy McCann for a while," I said.

She narrowed her eyes. "What do you know about that?"

I paused. I really had no business sticking my nose in here. After all, this was a decision that was made by Celeste and Connie, and there was a real possibility that my advice would be unwelcome. "Well, I know that you want to sell, and that Amy is probably the one who's going to come after you."

She nodded. "Yes, that's true. In fact, I'm meeting with her next week. Friday, I think. I have to check. At some lawyer's office, so I think she'll make a very good offer."

"You never mentioned it."

She shrugged her frail shoulders. "I didn't want to bother you, dear. There's really nothing else to be done. We need the money. Amy can get it for us. End of story."

Her coffee was strong and delicious, and that jam... "Listen, Celeste, you know what she'll probably do once she gets all this, right?"

Her eyes filled with tears. "Yes. She'll cut down all these beautiful trees. She'll drain my duck pond and make everything flat and concrete. This has been a little piece of heaven for me and Connie, but what else can I do?"

I reached across the table and took her hand. "If I could find another buyer who would give you a fair price but not bulldoze all the trees, and maybe even leave a few acres untouched, well, would you take that deal?"

She squeezed my fingers. "Of course. But honey, nobody likes to go up against Amy. She's very shrewd, you know." She leaned forward and dropped her voice. "She can be a real bitch."

I drew back, surprised. "You know her?"

Celeste shook her head. "No, but after I found out that Mike married her, well, I got curious and asked Marie Wu about her. Do you know Marie? Lovely woman, and so smart! Anyway, Marie told me all about her, and she sounded very...formidable."

"Yes, that's what I've heard as well. So, you've known Mike a long time?"

Her eyes glittered. "Since he was a kid, full of himself and thinking he could take on the world. He still has a rather high opinion of himself, but now he's earned it. He's a good man."

"Yes," I said. "I think so too."

"You like him," she said. "I could tell. What happened to that fellow you were living with?"

I shrugged. "I left him to take care of Mom."

She sighed. "I don't think you ever really loved him all that much. When you talked about him, you never had the kind of smile on your face that you had when you I saw you with Mike." She waggled her finger at me. "You can't tell me there's nothing going on there. I saw you two." She rapped her knuckles against the tabletop. "Chemistry."

I felt a smile. "Oh, really?"

"Oh, yes." She folded her hands and raised an eyebrow. "Are the two of you an item?"

I shook my head, aware that my cheeks were probably turning red. "No, Celeste. We're not."

She made a face. "Well, do something about that! And after being married to Amy, he deserves a good woman like you. I don't know why he married her in the first place." She leaned forward again. "I think she put the fix on him."

I was grinning now. "The fix?"

"She's a witch." She sat back. "She did something to him. Even he'll tell you. When I asked him why, he couldn't give me a reason."

"Maybe he was embarrassed to give you the reason?" I suggested. "Men do all sorts of things for, well..."

She threw back her head and cackled. "You might be right there, Christiana."

When we both stopped laughing, I took her hand again. "I think I know someone who could really do a wonderful job with this property. Can you wait? Maybe just a few weeks?"

She nodded. "Of, course, dear. We're paying the bills, and we can continue that. But I don't want Connie to be in that place any longer than necessary." She frowned and twisted her lips. "But what am I going to tell Amy? We haven't agreed to anything, but I'm sure she thinks she'll make an offer and...well, she's gonna be one pissed off lady if I try to shake her off."

Maybe it was all the caffeine. Maybe it was the sugar rush from the jam. "If Amy McCann gives you a hard time, you just send her to me, okay?"

She looked relieved, and a few of the wrinkles around her mouth smoothed out. "I will."

I drank some more of her delicious coffee. "Where will you go, Celeste? After you sell?"

She sighed and folded her hands. "There's a lovely assisted living place, just about twenty minutes north of here. I can buy a nice two-bedroom apartment. This place is quite nice. Bingo every Thursday, and bus trips, and when I visited them a while back, there were a bunch of people sitting around a piano and a very nice man was playing, the old songs, you know?" She grinned, showing crooked teeth. "And people do your laundry and cook your meals. I like that part. Of course, we can do our own cooking if we want, but never having to do laundry again?" Her smile broadened and she got a faraway look in her eyes. "That would be wonderful." She sighed again. "With money, things are good, yes?"

I felt so much better hearing her say that this is what she wanted, not just something she felt she had to do. "Yes. And you deserve it, Celeste. You and Connie both."

She cackled. "And it's close enough you can visit. You and Mike, okay? Now, let me get you another cup of coffee. I want you to tell me all about this house of yours."

So I did.

Chapter Five

Terri asked me sixteen times in the following days what was wrong with me and I kept on lying to her.

I didn't have to ask her how she knew something was wrong. I only had to look in the mirror. I was smiling. All the time. And it was a goofy, maybe-I'm-a-little-drunk kind of smile. I had the attention span of a gnat, because I was always staring off into space, imaging Mike and me in various situations; having dinner by the water, walking through the grounds of Eyre Hall, stretched out in front of my (nonexistent) fireplace. Each scenario, by the way, ended pretty much the same way, with the two of us naked. Terri, at one point, had to actually snap her fingers in front of my eyes, interrupting a very nice little scene where Mike and I were kissing in the sand, much like Burt Lancaster and Deborah Kerr in that very famous movie.

And I wasn't hungry.

I had spent the whole week walking down to the house and watching the work. I was at alternately fascinated and baffled. I knew there had to be a rhyme and reason to everything the men were doing and often tried to figure it out for myself. I asked Steve all sorts of questions and he was more than willing to answer them, so I actually learned quite a lot from him. He was charming and helpful and patient, as though I was going to take everything he said and actually put it to use in my real life. When Mike was on site, however, every time I asked him anything I found myself watching his mouth rather than listening to his words. From him I learned nothing except that his superpower was making me feel like a fifteen-year-old with a crush on the quarterback.

Keeping Terri at bay was the hardest part. I even went across the bridge on Sunday and saw three movies in a row so I wouldn't have to stay home with her and feel the crushing weight of her curiosity.

But I couldn't avoid the issue forever.

Finally, on Tuesday night, Buck A Beer night at DeeDee and Jacks, while barely eating a burger, Karen blew everything wide open. Terri had been on a bit of a rant, asking *why* I was in such a fog all the time, *why* I sat around with a silly smile on my face, *why* I wouldn't give her a straight answer...

"It sounds like she's in love," she said casually to Terri.

What a traitor. I was hoping she'd forgotten all about our little conversation about Mike, or that she had the decency to keep it to herself. But no, there she was, throwing it out to the world, and looking pretty pleased with herself as she did it. I kept my eyes down, reached for my beer, and hoped my cheeks had not gone completely red.

Terri froze in her seat and turned to me, very slowly. "It's Steve McCann, isn't it?" she whispered.

I almost spewed out my beer all over the table. "No!"

Stella patted me anxiously on the back and shook her head. "Terri, honey, you have got to stop thinking that Steve McCann is the only man in the world."

"Well who else could it be?" Terri demanded. "She already told me that Mike wasn't her type. Daniel? She ran into him once, but maybe that was all it took?" She looked at me suspiciously. "Unless you've been meeting him in secret?"

I shook my head. "No, Terri, I have not been meeting with Daniel in secret."

Terri took a deep breath "Well, I can completely understand if it is Steve. After all, he's just so good looking and charming...and you know, the women around here haven't had much luck with him, as far as any long-term commitments, and there are so many stories out there, but..."

"Terri, I am not in love with Steve McCann. And as for those stories, he told me not to pay too much attention to them."

She sat back and raised an eyebrow. "Oh, and when did he say that?"

"Right after I told him I wouldn't go out with him."

"What?" Her voice rose an octave. "He did what?"

"Oh..." I muttered into my burger and took a big bite, just to keep from saying anything else.

"And why didn't you tell me all this before?" Terri demanded.

I looked at Karen for help, chewing slowly.

"Terri, honey," Karen said gently, "obviously, since Chris didn't have any interest in Steve, she didn't say anything because she didn't want you to misinterpret the situation and get upset. And, obviously, her instincts were right."

"Oh." Terri folded her hands on the tabletop and frowned, a sign of deep thinking. "So you aren't in love with Steve?"

I shook my head.

"Or Daniel?"

I shook my head again.

"Well, then, who?"

I refocused on my burger.

"Well. Let's see." Stella's voice was bubbling with laughter. "Judd is gay, so I'm going to take a leap and say he's out."

Dara speared a fried shrimp with her fork and pointed it at me for emphasis. "I'm sure she's run into all sorts of men. Members of the construction crew? Maybe a shopkeeper? How about that person in the zoning office?"

I shuddered. "No," I said distinctly.

"Well, then," Karen said slowly, "I'm going to circle back to Mike."

Double traitor. I felt my face get hot, and I tried to tuck my chin onto my chest. Silence, as they say, fell.

"Listen guys, I am not in love with Mike McCann. And I'm sure," I said, a little louder than was probably necessary, "that he has no interest in me."

Dara sniffed. "You don't have to be so defensive. He's a very sexy man, in that rough-and-tumble teddy bear kind of way. I'd do him. If I did men, that is."

"I'm not being defensive," I snapped.

"Then why are you trying to convince us all that you don't like him, when you've obviously got some strong feelings about him," Terri said, reasonably. "Do you hate him?"

I stared at my burger. "No," I said roughly.

Karen sighed. "Well, then, there you go."

"He's completely *not* my type," I told them.

"Absolutely," Dara said, nodding her head.

"And he actually made fun of me, calling my ideas *big city*, like wanting to use a dresser in the bathroom was, like, a totally off-the-wall notion."

Stella smiled sympathetically. "I'm sure. So what are you going to do?"

I stared at her. "About what?"

"About Mike," she answered.

"Nothing!" I pushed away my plate. "I'm not going to do anything because, well...why should I?"

"Because there's obviously something going on," Terri said.

"Try cooking him a home cooked dinner," Stella said. "Men love a woman who cooks."

Dara elbowed her roughly. "Now, what the hell kind of 1954 advice to the lovelorn is *that*?"

Stella looked indignant. "A woman can be her own person, live her own life, and still be a good cook. And a man can believe in feminism, respect women, and appreciate a delicious meal. I'm just throwing out a suggestion here, not carving anything in stone."

"Right now, the only person I plan on cooking for is Celeste Montecorvo. I'm going to cook her a great big pot of Sunday sauce with meatballs and sausage and a huge hunk of pork, just as soon as I have a kitchen. And you all, of course. But I'm not cooking for Mike or any other man. I did not come to Cape Edwards to find a boyfriend, and I'm certainly not going to fall for the first guy in a beard and tool belt who happens to turn my legs to jelly." I picked up my burger and took another huge bite, hoping I'd be chewing it for the next hour, thereby logically preventing me from having to answer any more questions.

"Of course not," Karen said. "But maybe you could ask him for coffee? I bet if you have a nice, easy conversation with him, get to know him a bit better, away from the job site, I mean. You could easily sort out what you're feeling."

I glared at her. This was all her fault anyway, mentioning Mike in the first place. But as I chewed, I began to think maybe a nice, pleasant conversation would not be such a bad thing. We could talk. Of course we could. Just a simple, easy conversation, like we were having at the Coop before he had to go and touch me and send off all sorts of alarms. And as long as he didn't do anything too sexy, like run those long, strong fingers through his beard, smile that slightly evil smile or look at me too long with those gorgeous blue eyes...

Who was I kidding? Sitting there, just thinking about him, was getting me hot under the collar. Not to mention other places.

I finished my mouthful of burger. "I don't think it would be all that simple," I said.

"But it is," Karen said. "Send him a text. Ask him to meet you. He doesn't have to know why, does he? And when he shows up, just talk."

Just talk. She made it sound so easy. But then, she didn't know that while I would have loved to spend hours talking to Mike, what I'd really been thinking about doing with him actually involved not a whole lot of talking at all.

"I'll think about it," I said.

All around the table, my friends beamed, thinking they somehow solved my Mike problem.

If they only knew.

The next day, I sent Mike a text asking him to meet me for coffee. He texted back—*when*? I suggested nine thirty the next morning and he said okay.

It really was that easy. But I knew that he was going to assume I wanted to talk about the house. He was spending the day with Daniel and one of the subcontractors, discussing the parking lot of the project across the street. I knew that because, upon considering the building crew, I decided if I couldn't join them, I'd bribe them to at least not make faces and funny noises every time I set foot on the site. I started with brownies after the first week, individual apple tarts the next, and by now I not only knew all their names, but the names of their wives and kids as well.

My antique purchases had been delivered and were huddled in the middle of the bare plywood floor. Tyler, who still seemed to be too young to even drive, let alone manage the job while Steve and Mike were away, did not look pleased.

"Do you know about these?" he asked. He was holding a shortbread cookie in one hand and a nail gun in the other.

"Yes. Mike helped me pick them out, so they should all fit. This tall cupboard is going to be in the hall, for the closet. That dresser is going to be fitted for the bathroom vanity. And the table here is my kitchen island. I asked Steve to cancel the one we ordered with the cabinets."

Tyler nodded. "*That's* what's going in the hallway? We had to make a bit of an adjustment in the framing."

"That's done? Oh, good. Now it has to be stripped, sanded down, all those nails and things removed, and refinished. That's my project, by the way. You can just set it up, oh, anywhere."

He looked skeptical. "Your project?"

I nodded and handed him another cookie.

He chewed thoughtfully. "You ever strip varnish off anything before?"

I shook my head.

"Ever use a sander?"

I shook my head again. One side of my brain was getting all lofty and judgmental—I was a college-educated person, for heaven's sake. How hard could it be to use a sander? But the saner and calmer side of my brain knew, after binge watching hours of HGTV in the past few days, that those power tools could be tricky.

"I'll take it slow," I told him.

"Uh-huh."

"And Mike said he'd help me." That was not necessarily true. In fact, he hadn't said that at all, but I was pretty sure he would at least tell me what I was doing wrong.

Tyler rubbed his chin. "Well, Okay then. We still have a few days until drywall is finished. Alan has us roughed in, and the juice should be on by tomorrow. That way you can work on your, ah, project after, well..."

"After all of you guys have done the real work for the day?"

He grinned. "Yeah."

"Deal. I don't want to get in your way." I set the box of shortbread on the dresser. "Now, can I trust you to give these cookies to the rest of the crew?"

His grin broadened. "No."

"Well, at least you're honest. I don't suppose anything is happening today that I might actually be able to help you with?"

He looked at me critically. "What kind of help, exactly, do you think you can give?"

Terri and I had spent way too many nights together watching every TV show about flipping houses we could find and had carefully evaluated each and every step of the process.

"We could do that," she kept saying.

"No, Terri, neither of us can get up on a roof and nail shingles."

"We can do that," she suggested a few minutes later.

"Have you ever used a band saw before?"

"Well, we could probably do that."

"Terri, she's using a *blowtorch*."

My friend may have had a lofty opinion of her construction skills, but I knew mine were limited. Still, I wanted to show Tyler I was serious about this. "What about the baseboard? I can use a nail gun," I said, with much more confidence that I felt.

"Have to wait till all the drywall is up."

"Well..." I looked around. "I could do that! I can fill in all those holes with that white stuff."

I heard a cough behind me and felt the blood rush to my cheeks.

"You mean mud?" Mike walked up and turned to me, eyes twinkling. Joe was at his heels, sniffing the air.

I was not expecting him to be at the house. He was supposed to be in an office somewhere, talking about parking spaces. "Aren't you in a meeting with Daniel right now?" I asked, then immediately felt like an idiot. Of course he wasn't in a meeting, he was *standing* right there...

He grinned. "I knew they'd picked up your, ah, purchases from Celeste last night, and wanted to check to see that everything arrived here safely. Wouldn't want any unnecessary nicks or scratches on the merchandise."

I put my hands on my hips. "You're mocking me again, aren't you?"

He shook his head, and I could see him fighting a smile. "Nope. Not me. And everything looks just fine."

"And I could absolutely help with...mud." Right. Mud. I knew that. I'd been around houses and builders and renovators for years, I knew what mud was...why did I have to look like a total idiot in front of Mike? Why did I *have to feel* like an idiot? I dropped my hands from my hips and wiped my palms against my sides. "And even if I didn't know *what* to do, I am teachable, you know."

His face softened. "You are absolutely right. In fact, you are one smart woman. But being smart and knowing what to do around a job site are very different things. Just because Tyler here looks and acts like an ignorant fool doesn't mean he isn't in possession of a finely developed set of skills, all necessary to rebuilding a house. Ain't that right, Tyler?"

Tyler, obviously enjoying the show, nodded.

Mike looked suddenly serious. "Where did you get that cookie," he demanded.

Tyler pointed to me, and I pointed to my offering, cookies in a shoebox. Joe sat and immediately lifted one paw.

Mike took one, bit, chewed carefully, then nodded with approval. "You baked these?"

"Terri has a very nice kitchen," I said.

"So," he said, reaching for another, "You been feeding my boys?"

"Her brownies," Tyler said with obvious sincerity, "were amazing."

Mike nodded again, broke off a bit of cookie, and tossed it to Joe, who caught gift midair. "Well, Chris, maybe you do know more about work crews than I gave you credit for. Let me just explain to Tyler here where all of these exquisite antiques are going, and I'll be on my way. But first..." he reached over and took another cookie. "These are excellent."

"She said you were going to help her? With this?" Tyler pointed to my future hall closet/armoire.

"Well, sure, I'll be happy to help," Mike said easily. "After all, if she chokes on the fumes from the stripping solution and dies, my insurance will go through the roof." He winked at me. "I got your back, Chris. Don't worry."

I felt myself turning red again and hurried out the front door. Good heavens. If I was going to turn into a blushing fool every time I was in the same room as him...

Mike stuck his head out the front door. "Hey, listen, we're still meeting tomorrow?"

I nodded.

"Nothing we can't talk about now?"

I shook my head.

"Alrighty then. See you."

I sat on my new front steps and watched the traffic going toward the beach. I felt ridiculously pleased with myself because he liked my cookies. Maybe I could bake a chocolate cake and bring it to him in the morning...

Judd had texted me to ask if there was progress, and if he could stop by and take pictures. I'd texted back yes, and waited, and while I waited I thought, and the more I thought, the more frustrated I became.

I was a fool. Mike was the kind of man who probably made every single woman he came in contact with feel the way I felt now: flustered, charmed, bothered and flattered. He was a natural flirt. He flirted with me. He probably flirted with a lot of women. Why on earth did I think that maybe, just maybe, I was special to him? Especially since he had apparently sworn off *all* women?

Because there was a spark. I felt it. And I was old and wise enough to recognize it for what it was.

All I had to do now is get Mike to admit that he felt it too.

But...did I want this? Did I want to get involved with a man right now? Wasn't it enough that I was moving to a new place, building a new house, trying to put together a new life...how much more complicated did I want my life to be? I mean, talk about taking risks...

Karen was right. All I needed to do was sit and spend a little time with him, and all the confusing and, admittedly, lustful thoughts would sort themselves out and I'd see clearly that he was not the kind of guy I needed in my life, especially not right now.

Judd pulled up in front of the house and came up the walk.

"Lots of progress?" he asked.

I got up and led him through. The framing was complete, the electric had been roughed in and drywall was going up everywhere. Pipes poked out of the rough floor, showing where my kitchen sink would be, and my washer hookup, and more pipes were sticking out in the bathroom. You could visualize the spaces now.

He seemed particularly interested in the pieces I'd bought from the Coop.

"These can be part of the before and after," he said. "They're perfect."

He obviously knew more about the construction process than I, because when he asked Tyler questions about the progress, Tyler did not roll his eyes in complete disgust. He took some pictures, and in about fifteen minutes, we were back on the sidewalk.

"You're making good progress," he said. "With the house, anyway. How are you?"

How was I? Confused, bothered, feeling lustful...oh, maybe he wasn't talking about me in terms of Mike McCann. "Good."

He looked across the street. "So, your ex is right there?"

"Boy," I said, "the jungle drums around here are pretty impressive."

He laughed. "Especially when it comes to the new girl in town who not only bought the Farnham place, but dances on the beach naked."

I shook my head. "That was two years ago, and it will not be repeated."

"That's a shame. Folks around here just love that kind of stuff." He glanced over slyly. "And you've been seen with both of those McCann brothers."

I kept my eyes down. "They're building my house. Of course I've been seen with them."

He chuckled. "Too bad. A love triangle would have really spiced things up around here."

I laughed. "Sorry, Judd."

He sighed. "How disappointing."

Terri was trying to give me advice. "Maybe you should blow out your hair?"

Ridiculous. My hair was the perfect combination of my Italian father and Irish mother: fair, not at all blonde but not quite brown, with a smidge of red highlights, and all thick and curly and impossible to manage in heat or humidity. "That will last six minutes in this heat," I told her. "I'll scrunch the curls with lots of mousse and hope for the best.

"Maybe a dress?"

"I'm meeting him for coffee at Shorty's, not cocktails at Sam's on Main."

"Then wear shorts. You've got great legs."

Also, short legs. Most shorts I bought ended up as Bermudas, even if they were sold as Daisy Dukes.

I found my denim skirt and a sleeveless linen blouse, a dark red, which looked good with my olive skin and dark eyes.

"Perfect," Terri said. She had settled in the middle of my bed, her back against the headboard, drinking a glass of wine. "So, listen. I think we should buy another property to redo."

I was looking at myself critically in the mirror. My boobs were starting to sag, and I squinted at the soft pooch around my stomach. Surely, that hadn't been there the last time I wore this skirt. I untucked the shirt and pulled it down over the waistband, hiding the slight bulge. Better. "What did you just say?"

"There are all sorts of places around here we can buy and fix up and sell for loads of money."

I turned sideways and sucked in my stomach. There. Not only did my front flatten out, my boobs actually perked up a bit "Wait...loads of money?"

"I think we should buy a house and flip it and make that our business."

I turned and looked at her, my eyes narrowing. "Terri, honey, you haven't even gotten around to lifting a hammer on this project. What makes you think you could do this on a regular basis? What *is* this?"

She shrugged. "We could get the McCann brothers to help us out again, and—"

"Oh, I get it. All part of your ongoing plan to have Steve McCann fall in love with you?"

She grinned. "You bet."

I shook my head. "Terri, why don't you just find out where he lives and show up at his front door wearing nothing but your birthday suit?"

She rolled her eyes. "I don't want to seem obvious, Chris. Yeesh, give me a break."

"Can we at least wait and see how my house turns out before we try another fixer-upper? This really isn't as easy as it looks on HGTV, you know. Those people on television have been doing this sort of thing for a long time. And besides, we need to figure out how to pay for another project, which means you're going to have to find a little seed money of your own."

She frowned, obviously thinking that one through. "You've got a point," she said at last. "But let's at least look around at a few, just to see what's out there."

I sighed. "Okay, if you find something, I'll go with you, but only to look."

She hopped off the bed. "Good. I need to get ready for bed. I also need to watch some more HGTV. My vacation starts in two weeks, and I'm going to spend all my time at the house. I should try to learn *something*, right?"

"Well, I've got dibs on the drywall," I said.

She leaned down and planted a sloppy kiss on my cheek. "You are the bestest of friends, you know that?"

"And you are the most annoying of friends."

"Yes, but you still love me, right?"

I sighed. "Yes. And I'll see a house if it looks really worthwhile. But no promises, Okay? I'm just going to look."

She beamed. "Of course! And no pressure. I promise."

Right.

Chapter Six

Somehow, in the time between trying on a denim skirt and looking totally adorable, and actually walking out of the door in it, I gained twenty-three pounds and aged at least six years. Also my hair turned into a Brillo pad. And I think the color of my eyes may have changed.

"Why do I look so terrible?" I whispered to myself the next morning. Listen, I never thought I was a raving beauty, but I thought I looked pretty good for a fifty-year-old. Now, even if I upped the age by ten, I'd be pushing it.

"You look fine," Terri said as she went out the door, showered, dressed and ready for work. She was lying, of course. What did she know of it anyway? She had a smoking body for a woman of any age, her hair still looked the same soft, pretty blond it had been in college, despite the gray, and she had acquired exactly three wrinkles, all in the corner of one blue eye.

I waved at her as she left then returned to the mirror.

Was that a wart on my chin? I leaned closer. A smudge on the mirror, thank God, but I wouldn't have been surprised.

I glanced at the clock. Could I find a spa open at seven twenty in the morning that would completely redo my face and body in less than two hours?

Then, I straightened my spine and remembered that I wasn't fifteen anymore. And what did I care what I looked like? I wasn't out to impress Mike McCann. I just wanted to talk to him. I was hoping to find a logical reason for all those crazy feelings I kept getting around him. I did not believe in love at first sight. Or second or even third sight. Yet here I was, practically peeling off my clothes every time I even thought about the man, and I barely knew him. Maybe a nice long talk would put things in perspective.

I just wasn't all that sure I wanted things in perspective. After all, if I was going to start taking risks...

I sat at my computer and answered some emails, made a few phone calls that had to do with my old real estate office and the upcoming sale of Mom's house, and managed to watch half an episode on HGTV that showed a tiny woman demolishing an entire wall with a sledge-hammer and a smile. I was beginning to think that HGTV should be renamed the Fantasy Network.

At nine fifteen I was ready to head down the street. I took one more look at myself in the mirror, decided that Spanx and a little lipstick wouldn't hurt, and headed out five minutes later.

Mike had grabbed a table on the sidewalk and was reading the newspaper when I got there. Joe was at his feet and lifted his head as I approached and wagged his tail.

"Did I keep you waiting?" I asked.

He lowered the paper and smiled. "No. Sometimes I show up here all by myself, just to read and have a cup. Coffee? Or something cute and frothy?"

I raised an eyebrow. "I didn't think I came off as the cute and frothy type."

"Welp, you don't, but I'm trying to scale back on my snap judgments of people, so I thought I'd ask."

The waitress fluttered over, took my order for coffee and a sweet roll, and hurried off.

"Now, see?" Mike said, eyes twinkling. "If I was the type to make snap judgments, I'd take one look at your legs and think, now, there's a woman who watches every single thing she eats. And, obviously, I'd be wrong."

I laughed. "I was born with amazing metabolism, and thank God." He thought I had nice legs. And here I'd been beating myself about looking fat. If nothing else, that sentence alone was worth all the morning's angst.

He folded his paper and set it on his lap. "Thank God, indeed. Now, what was it you wanted to talk about?"

I went through about sixteen possible answers, then decided to try the truth. "You. I mean, just...stuff. I think it would help our, you know, working relationship if I knew you a bit better."

He sat back, looking surprised and amused. "Really?"

Coffee and a sweet roll appeared, and he watched as I stirred in sugar and cream and took a tiny bite off the edge of the roll. Delicious. I broke off a piece and lowered my hand. Joe sidled over and delicately took it from my fingertips.

Mike watched Joe, then lifted his eyes to me. "Well, what do you want to know?"

I wanted to know how those long, graceful fingers would feel trailing down my bare back. I wanted to know if that beard would be bristly or soft. I wanted to know how those lips would taste...

"How do you know Celeste?"

He sat back, chuckling. "Well, she and Connie have always made their own wine. They grew grapes, stomped them, bottled them, and word got out that one sip of their homemade concoction would set you back on your butt, and fast. I was only seventeen and figured that stealing bottle or two from them would be easier than trying to fool the guy at the liquor store, so I snuck in their back shed one night and tried to commit the crime of the century." He shook his head. "Connie caught me by the belt loop as I was trying to climb through the window and nearly ripped me a new one. We made a deal. She wouldn't tell my father in exchange for a bit of hard labor in their garden. My dad, well, he would have grounded me for the rest of my natural life, so I thought it was a sweet deal. Those little ladies worked my tail end off that summer, but they fed me good, and the next summer, I went back." He shook his head again. "They love their little piece of land the way some folks love their families. They walked it every day, talked about the trees, and they planted things everywhere—little wildflower gardens in the middle of nowhere, more vines for wine, rose bushes in patches of sunlight."

Oh, he was such a nice guy to realize that about the two of them. I felt my face burst into a smile. "I know. I've walked that ground with them. And I've tasted their wine. I ask for it over a tall glass of ice, that's the only way I can drink it. That is a great story. So, you've known them for a really long time?"

He raked his fingers through his beard. "You didn't have to put so much emphasis on the *really*, but yes, I certainly have. I manage to stay in touch with them, even when I was in Boston. I don't get to spend as much time with Celeste now, just too busy. But I did see Connie a few months back. She's not...happy where she is."

"I talked to Celeste last week. She gave me the whole scoop: selling the property, moving into assisted living with Connie...she's got her new place already picked out, and it sounds nice."

"I know where she's talking about, and it is nice. I'm thinking about signing up there right now, you know, planning for the future." There was that grin again. "All it takes is money."

"Which they will certainly have, but, well, I convinced her to put off your, ah, ex-wife." I said, breaking off another piece of roll for Joe.

"You *what?*" His eyes popped open.

"I think Daniel should buy the property. Has he told you about his build-a-village idea? That property would be perfect. I just need to talk him into it."

He raised an eyebrow. "Daniel? I had the feeling this project on Main was going to be a one-off deal."

"Maybe. Daniel changes his mind quite frequently, especially about his business dealings. I've seen him walk away from a project after months of negotiations, and then turn around and invest millions on a pitch at a cocktail party. If I can convince him that he could make money—and win the approval of the entire county to boot—by keeping some of the land as green space, I think he'll go for it."

"I know that Celeste and Connie would really love to see some-body take that property and try to save a bit of what they loved about it. And I know that Amy is not that person." He shook his head and pursed his lips. "Definitely not that person. Well, he's back next week, so go ahead and make the pitch."

"I will. Celeste was a little worried about putting Amy off, so I told her if there was any problem, to send Amy to me."

"*WHAT?*" His jaw dropped. "You told her to send Amy...are you *kidding*? Do you have any idea what that could mean?"

I have to say I was a bit taken aback. "I guess maybe I don't," I said slowly.

Mike settled back and covered his eyes with his hand, shaking his head. "Oh, my goodness. Well, if that does happen, please call me, because where ever I am, and whatever I'm doing, that is something I really want to see."

"Mike, if she's as awful as everyone says she is, then why did you marry her?" The words popped out of my mouth, and there was nothing I could do to jump after them and try to drag them back where they belonged.

He took a deep breath. "When I was in Boston, I was with a terrific woman for years. We never married because, well, because we never did. When I lost my job, I asked her to come down here with me, but she had her own life, a great career, her family was there...so she stayed and I left and it was hard. I was just starting the business with Steve, feeling totally sorry for myself, and then I ran into Amy at some business breakfast and..." He looked away, as though trying to find the right words.

"She and I...well, you know that old song, about getting married in a fever? That was us. We met, and there was a, ah, certain chemistry. When she said we should get married, I thought it was the best idea I'd ever heard. Eventually, we had to get out of bed and start talking to each other, and that's when the problems began. Luckily, we hadn't been together long enough to warrant anything more than a simple, do-it-yourself divorce. We still see each other from time to time, but when it happens, I'm usually walking very quickly in the opposite direction." He grinned. "Steve will still give me a hard time about it, every once in a while. But he knows better than to mention her too often."

"He did mention her, when we were talking about the Coop. And Daniel mentioned her too, when we were talking about his interest in the area."

"I like Daniel," Mike said.

"I do too. But the last few years we were together it was just that. Like. I think we stayed a couple out of habit more than anything else."

He looked at me steadily. "That happens to people. He told me about your mom. I'm sorry."

I felt a rush of tears. It happened, sometimes, just when I thought I was over her death and everything was back to normal. "Thank you."

"He's very surprised that you're here. He told me he couldn't imagine you just leaving Rehoboth and buying a house, just off the cuff like that."

They had talked about me? Really. Whose idea was that? Was it because Mike curious?

"Daniel is right. This is unusual for me. After my mother died, the only thing left for me in Rehoboth was a career I was starting to feel very ambivalent about, so I decided to try living my life...differently. I'm taking a few risks now, doing things I never would have even thought about before. Like buying a house I've never seen." *Or like falling hard for Mike McCann*, I thought. "It's scary, but so far it seems to be paying off."

He reached over, picked up his coffee mug and took a long drink, watching me over the rim of the cup. When he set it down, he said, "Hear you went to lunch out at Curry's last week. How did you like that blue-ribbon service?"

I had to think for a second. "Curry's? Is that where Steve took me? Best crab cake sandwich I think I've ever had, but your brother had to practically bludgeon the waiter into bringing me another glass of water."

He laughed. "Yeah, that sounds about right. It's one of Steve's favorite places." He was watching me carefully. "He likes to bring his women there."

I tore my eyes from his and focused on my sweet roll. I broke off a piece and chewed carefully. "It was just lunch," I said. I leaned across the table. "But he asked me out, and I really haven't talked to him since. Is there going to be a problem? I mean, with the house?"

Mike shook his head. "No. Don't worry about that. Steve, well, he loves women. Loves the way they look and what they say. Especially what they do. But, he doesn't really *like* them. And he doesn't get... attached. So I'm sure he's over it by now. He may take another stab at it, but that's just his way. But he did mention it. See, he doesn't get turned down very often. And he seemed...intrigued by your refusal." His eyes were bright. "Why did you say no?"

What could I say? That although Steve was a perfectly nice and quite good-looking man, he was not the McCann I was interested in?

This was the moment. I could look Mike straight in the eye and tell him that the McCann I *really* wanted was...

But it was just too much. I gulped. "I told him that I was just getting my footing around here and wanted to stick with my women friends and concentrate of getting my life in order."

He nodded. "Yes. I was just wondering...well." He folded his hands on his lap, and I felt it. A change in his attitude. A second before he had been interested, perhaps even eager. Now, there was an air detachment to him.

Perfect. If he had any interest in me at all, I just told him to forget it, because I wasn't going to be dating anyone anytime soon. Was it too late? Could I summon the nerve and just open my mouth and take the chance?

The moment had passed, but I had to get us back on some sort of track. Anything that would get us together, away from the house and away from Steve. Luckily, we had the love of old junk in common. "So, about the house. I'd love to find crystal doorknobs. Those old-fashioned kind? And maybe some leaded or stained glass to put in the bathroom window for privacy. And I really want a headboard for my bed, something really cool...maybe craftsman? I love that style."

His expression brightened. "I know just the place for that kind of stuff. Just north here, not far. You could drive up some weekend."

I took a mental deep breath and took the step. "Why don't you come with me? I'd probably come home with a carload of all the wrong sizes."

His eyes narrowed. "Sure. Busy this Saturday?"

I shook my head. "Nope. My big plan was cutting the grass."

"Well, we can head on up Onancock and take a look around."

Gotcha. "Really? Thanks. That would be great."

He pushed his coffee mug to the center of the table. "Well, Chris, this was nice, and it looks like we've got a hot shopping expedition to look forward to. But right now I've got to go and try to fix a roof that is literally hanging by a thread, and the client doesn't understand that an estimate is just that, and not anything written in stone. Wish me luck."

I waved. "Luck," I said, and watched his and Joe walk down toward the water.

Damn him anyway. I was pretty sure that maybe, just maybe he *was* exactly the kind of man for me.

And I had pretty much just told him I was not looking for any kind of man at all.

I spent all day filling little dents with goopy white stuff, then smoothing with the side of a tool that looked like a very short-handled pancake flipper.

The dents were caused by the drywall screws anchoring the drywall to the two-by-fours that were the walls to my house. Apparently, you needed about six thousand screws per sheet of drywall. Okay, maybe not that many, but it sure seemed like that many. The seams between the sheets of drywall also had to be filled and smoothed, but it was obvious that my skill set was nowhere near where it needed to be for that particular task. So I stuck the corner of my flipper into the mud, filled the dent, turned the flipper over, and applied enough pressure to remove all the goop except just the amount needed to create a smooth surface.

I did not wear my old clothes, didn't cover my hair, and didn't wear my work boots. So at the end of the day, there were flecks of white all over my nice cotton shorts—and my legs—as well as in my hair, on my arms, and down the front of my T-shirt. Don't ask. I also stubbed eight out of ten toes against various bits of lumber, various ladders, large buckets of mud...

Right about the time I was ready to throw my spackle knife into Tyler's grinning face, Steve showed up, did a quick walk-through, then stopped in front of me, smiling.

"Chris, I have to say, you've surprised me here. Lots of homeowners say they want to do and learn, but you're about the first I've met who's actually shown up and done all the work. Why don't we go out and get a nice cold drink? You look like you could use a little de-stressing."

First of all, what I probably looked like was a hot mess in need of a steam cleaning, not a cold drink. And this was absolutely him asking me out. I thought we'd gotten over that, but apparently not.

"Thanks, Steve, but look at me. I need hosed off."

He laughed. "I'll grant you that. How about I meet you then? Later sometime tonight?"

Oh, why was he such a nice man? And so good looking? And why was he not interested in Terri? And what was he going to tell his brother this time?

I shook my head. "I'm already all aches and pains. And I'm not used to this—I'll probably be asleep by seven thirty. Besides," I said, knowing he'd hear about it anyway, "I have to get up pretty early tomorrow. Mike and I are on a doorknob hunt."

He made a face. "Yeah that sounds about right for Mike. He loves all that junk. Okay, but maybe next time?"

What was I supposed to say? I shook my head. "I don't think so, Steve. Like I said, I'm just trying to get my feet under me, and..."

He held up a hand. "Yes. I know. Sorry." He looked at me. "Didn't mean to push. I just think you're an interesting and attractive woman, Chris. That's all."

I knew I was blushing and was grateful for the coating of drywall dust that covered my skin. "And I'm flattered. Really."

He nodded, as though to himself, then flashed a smile. "Have a good weekend. I hope you find your doorknobs."

I watched him go with a sinking heart. Perfect. Next time he and Mike got together over a beer, Steve would be sure to tell him how I still wasn't ready to be dating anyone, Mike would probably slap him on the back in sympathy, and take one giant step further away from me.

Unless I could do something tomorrow to change his mind.

Needless to say, I completely blew off all Friday night activities and soaked in a tub for almost an hour before falling asleep on the couch, my head still wrapped in a towel, by eight thirty.

Terri was nice enough to help me to bed when she came in from the pier.

When I woke up, muscles I never knew I had were screaming at me, asking what the hell was I doing to them after fifty years of devoted service, and begging, please, don't ever do it again.

"I swear, all I did was stand and spackle," I muttered to Terri as I washed down Aleve with very sweet coffee.

"And when was the last time you did that?" she asked, arching her eyebrows over the rim of her mug.

"Never," I muttered. "Just you wait till you spend your vacation over there. I'm betting you'll be hurting. God, when did we get old?"

"This has nothing to do with age," she said with conviction. "It has everything to do with your body being completely not used to manual labor. If you'd been alive two hundred years ago and spent all your days hauling wood and washing clothes in a river, you wouldn't feel a twinge."

"If I'd been alive two hundred years ago," I muttered, "I know I would have been one of those people the settlers would have happily traded to the Indians. Hauling wood my ass."

She burst out laughing. "I have to breakfast. Enjoy your day."

"I will. And tell all the ladies I said hello, and one of these Saturdays I'm going to join you."

She trotted out, and I finished my cereal, drank more coffee, and waited until the Aleve started to work, then got dressed and ready to meet Mike.

He picked me up in a two-seater, a tiny convertible sports car that looked like it belonged in a 1960s spy movie. I stood at the curb and stared. I never would have imagined him with a car quite like this.

He waved me in. "Don't look shocked. I'm a man of many facets."

Obviously. "What kind of car is this?" I asked as I buckled myself in.

"Austin-Healey Sprite," he said. "My baby."

"I can't help but notice there's no back seat or truck space. If we want to buy something, there's no way to get it home."

He grinned. "Exactly."

I had to hold my hat on my head the whole drive up, but it was worth it to feel the breeze on my face. Driving in a top-down convertible wasn't very conducive to conversation. After a few attempts of shouting over the road noise, I just sighed happily and looked at the scenery. We arrived in Onancock just before noon, and Mike parked on a side street.

"Eat then walk?" He asked.

I nodded. "Mike, if you spend any time with me at all, you'll know that if there's a choice between eating and anything else, eating comes first."

He took me to a building right on the water that had been a general store, and I ate crab and scallops and sweet tea, and then we walked around town, stopping in a few art galleries before arriving at the antique market, which proved pleasant enough, and fairly safe, until we walked all the way through and came across a treasure trove of architectural salvage pieces. I looked, mouth open, and sighed happily.

"Mike, would you look at all this stuff?"

He was grinning. "I had a feeling this would be the place for you. Remember, we can't bring anything home bigger than hinges or maybe a doorknob or two."

Actually, we brought home enough doorknobs for the entire house, as well as hooks to hang bathroom towels, a rectangular piece of ironwork to hang from the ceiling on the porch, and hinges for the new screen door. We did not find any stained glass, and he did manage to talk me out of a few items.

"Chris, I know this mantle is beautiful, but you don't have a fireplace."

"I know, but I could use it as a headboard in the guest room."

"Another big-city-designer idea?"

"Stop that. It's a very common design idea and you know it. And how about this?"

"It's a milk separator. You planning on making cheese?"

"But it's so *cool*..."

The man saved me a fortune. But looking around at all the things that wouldn't work for my house, I started thinking about what I could do if I *did* renovate another house. Hmm.

On the way back we stopped at Eyre Hall, one of my favorite places in the world, and we walked through the late afternoon sun to the creek, then sat, perfectly and happily quiet. I could hear other people in the gardens, and the sound of their voices mixed with the chirping of the birds and the quiet song of the water.

"This was a good day," he said at last.

"Yes, it was." We were not touching. We weren't even sitting that close, but I had never felt so aware of a man's body before. He was leaning forward, his forearms resting on his thighs, hands clasped. I could see glints of silver and gray among the dark brown hairs on his arms and the fabric of his knit shirt stretched across his shoulders. I was thinking that I could just run my fingers lightly across the top of his shoulders, and down the center of his broad back...

"So, listen, if you're still interested in some kinda glass thing for your bathroom, Steve is looking at a probable tear-down this week. The house, what's left of it, is pretty old, so I'll ask him to keep an eye out."

I cleared my throat. "That would be good. Thanks."

He sat back and stretched his arm out along the back of the bench seat. If I leaned far back enough, I could rest the base of my neck right along his bare arm...

"The doorknobs we got today? Now, they're a real find. Gonna fit just fine. Lucky for you we saved all those old doors of yours, because they were just about the only things in good shape. Can't beat a solid pine door like that. We've already stripped 'em down, and they have a nice stain on them. The knobs should be easy, and they'll look just fine. The hinges, now, you're gonna have to clean them up. It's a dirty job. No, maybe just messy. You up for it?"

"Why wouldn't I be?" I asked, as I imagined leaning over and turning his face to mine. His lips looked soft. I bet they tasted just like...

"Well, I know how you city girls are about getting your manicures ruined."

I sat up. "I do not get manicures," I told him. "And that's the second time you called me a city girl. Rehoboth is not exactly a metropolis, you know."

"True, but compared to Cape Edwards, it may as well be the Big Apple."

"You know, Mike," I said, feeling a little annoyed, "You lived most of your adult life in Boston, which is not some trivial New England burg. When are you going to stop with the small-town BS? You're not fooling me, you know."

"I told you, you can't take the Eastern Shore out of the man."

I frowned. Just when I was thinking some pretty positive things about him, including how nice it would be to maybe feel those soft lips against mine, he had to go all *aw, shucks* on me, and he *knew* I knew it was all an act.

"And I have no problem with hard work and you know it. I spackled yesterday."

He nodded. "Yep. Heard all about it. Tyler said you were pretty much covered from head to foot."

"Yeah, well, it was my first time! I bet the first times you ever tried some things, it wasn't perfect."

He turned to me, eyes twinkling. "Well, I hate to boast, but most of my first times are fairly spectacular."

I had no reply. I'm fairly certain that my mouth was hanging open and I could feel the color rush to my face.

I didn't know whether to kiss him or smack him upside the head.

I huffed and bolted off the bench. I could hear him behind me, making some sort of noise, but I didn't care. If only he would stop with all that teasing, and pretending that I was some fragile flower that might get a splinter or break a nail if I did anything...

I whirled, and he was so close behind me that we bumped before he jumped back about a foot. But that bump did it. My skin felt on fire and I knew my cheeks were red, and all I could think about was reaching up and grabbing him by the shirt and kissing him...

"What are you so touchy for?" he grumbled. "I'm only teasing."

"Well, don't," I snapped. "I mean, is that the only way you know how to relate to women? By teasing and making fun, and, and, well, you know." I waved my hands in the air, but I don't think it helped me get my point across.

He put both hands up in front of him, as though surrendering to a posse. "I'm sorry. You're right. I should not be mocking you, your hard work, or any of your efforts. In fact, I want to thank you for taking such a interest, and doing all that hard work."

Well...that was better. "You're welcome."

The air between us was practically crackling. Couldn't he feel it?

"I usually don't relate to women at all," he said, dropping his hands. "That's Steve's area of expertise."

"Yeah, well, I wish he'd stop asking me out," I mumbled.

Mike looked suddenly serious. "Is he bothering you?"

"What? No, not at all. He's perfectly polite. It's just, well..."

"I know. And I get it, Chris, I really do. It's hard enough moving to a new place, trying to build a new house, all with your ex-boyfriend camping across the street."

I shook my head. "Daniel has nothing to do with it," I said.

"Well, maybe, maybe not. You two were together long time. And he told me he didn't want to let you go."

I rolled my eyes. "And did he also tell you that he's moved on?"

"Oh, yeah, but he said that Chloe wasn't the kind of woman for the long term."

My jaw dropped open. "Chloe? From his office Chloe? She just signed on as an intern a few months before I left."

Mike's eyes started to twinkle. "He did say she worked with him. A little jealousy there?"

"Are you kidding? No. Just complete and absolute shock. She was his *intern*. That makes her barely legal." Oh Daniel, I thought. Sure, we hadn't exactly been setting the world on fire those last years together, but for him to latch on to Chloe, who could barely have a conversation about anything she didn't find on Instagram...

He laughed, and as he did the tension in the air faded away. "That's probably what he meant."

We started walking back to the car, not talking. Not touching either, but I knew exactly where his body was, slightly behind mine as we walked out to his truck. We sat in silence the short trip back, and he pulled up in front of Terri's.

"Like I said, this was a good day."

I felt like I was jumping out of my skin. I had to do something, say something...

"Thanks for coming with me," I mumbled, and reached over and gave him a quick kiss on the cheek. Then, coward that I was, I jumped out of the truck and practically ran up the stairs to Terri's.

So much for taking chances. I could have just as easily taken his face in both my hands and let him know exactly how good a day it was, but chickened out.

I was going to seriously have to work on that, or I'd never have a chance with him at all.

Chapter Seven

My house was finally *looking* like a house. There was a floor —plywood, but solid. Rooms were framed and there was drywall everywhere. All the electrical things were sticking out: sockets, switches, wires dangling from the beams, and various holes on the ceilings and walls. Roughed in, Tyler explained. We were all hooked up and waiting for the inspector so the Alan could finish his work and actually bring power into the house. Tyler had my tall kitchen cabinet-armoire-future-hall-closet standing in the middle of what would be my new living room and said I could pretty much do everything I needed to do, except use an electric sander.

I had everything I needed: stripper, an approved container to put the stripper into (apparently there were rules that dealt with safety that the nice clerk at Home Depot explained to me but I didn't understand), two brand new tarps, a metal brush, a few small paint brushes, denatured alcohol, latex gloves, disposable face masks and sandpaper in every available grit known to man. I also had metal paint scrapers in three sizes. With the money I'd spent at Home Depot, I could have had a custom cabinet built. In mahogany.

Tyler looked at my little pile and smiled. "Got enough stuff?"

I had watched no less than six videos of YouTube. He wasn't about to intimidate me. I knew exactly what I was doing.

He helped me spread out the tarps, not questioning why I had two, which was good, because I didn't want to explain. In my mind, paint stripper was the equivalent of hydrochloric acid and I was afraid if I spilled any, it would eat through everything and leave a gaping hole in the new plywood floor.

Then we lifted the cabinet right in the middle of the tarp(s) and he grinned.

"Good luck."

The first thing I needed to do, I realized with a sinking heart, was remove the doors. For that I needed a screwdriver, which I didn't have, but Tyler graciously lent me one. The rest of the crew watched but at least no one smirked—that mornings offering had been chocolate cupcakes.

Then I saw that the hardware had been painted over with paint so many times that it was impossible to see where to put the screwdriver. I figured that one out myself and used a bit of stripper, dabbing it on then springing back, waiting for it to explode.

It didn't.

After about twenty minutes I took a closer look, and sure enough, the paint had been miraculously melted away. However, the screws weren't Philip's head screws, they were the plain, old-fashioned kind.

Luckily, Tyler had that kind of screwdriver too.

So, I unscrewed the hinges from the doors, laid the doors, which were surprisingly heavy, on the tarp(s), then unscrewed the hinges from the body of the cabinet. Then I pulled out the three drawers at the bottom, ignoring the broken pulls. That left me with a big open box with four firmly attached shelves, which had been painted over approximately one hundred times.

Okay, maybe not that many, but it sure looked that way.

By now, I was hot and sweaty and the hair was sticking all down the back of my neck. I was also exhausted and had to pee.

I told Tyler I'd be back and walked down to Terri's. I was sure that the Jonny-On-The-Spot out back was just fine, but...

While I was there, I drank a gallon of water, stood in front of the air-conditioner, peed again and walked back. I contemplated changing clothes and maybe doing something with my hair in case Mike walked over, but I knew that after ten minutes in the heat I'd be a sweaty mess again, so I settled for washing my face and hoping he was too busy across the street to come by.

Back at the house, I found a few scrap pieces of two-by-four and put them under the cabinet doors, lifting them up off the tarp(s), and poured a bit of stripper on the raised panel of the first door. I carefully spread it, using the paintbrush, as per the directions on the container and four of the six videos I'd seen.

I backed away and watched and sure enough, things happened. I could see the paint lifting up and off the surface of the wood. I slowly and carefully scraped away, disposing the still toxic, possible deadly gunk in an approved container, and lo and behold, there was wood. Soft, brown wood, with a pale grain running all the way down. I sat back and grinned. I felt like I'd given birth. I was exhilarated, exhausted, starving...I glanced around. The house was empty. I looked at my phone and saw that it was almost one o'clock. Everyone was at lunch.

I walked home, ate, cooled off, and sat for a minute on the couch. I resisted the urge to just stretch out, because I knew if I did, I'd be fast asleep.

Back at the house, the crew was there, and Tyler was standing over my work, looking surprised.

"Hey, this is going to look good," he said as I walked up.

"Don't sound so surprised," I said. "Of course it's going to look good." I took a picture of my progress with my phone and sent it to Mike, then stooped down to work on the second door.

It was hot. I seriously thought about putting the whole project on hold until Alan came and finished his work, we passed the electrical inspection, and I could turn on the air-conditioning. But I looked around and saw the crew working away, most of them with their T-shirts plastered to their bodies with sweat. If they could work in the heat, so could I. But, I was older than all of them and felt no guilt about walking back to Terri's, changing into yet another sleeveless shirt, drinking lots of cold water while standing under the air-conditioning vent, and even splashing cold water all over my face after I peed. Twice.

Back at the house, Mike was there, hands on his hips, looking down at the doors. As I walked in, he grinned, and Joe actually trotted up to me for a welcoming sniff.

"So, I see you're hard at work," he said, his eyes twinkling.

I felt a little punch in my gut. Working in the heat looked a whole lot better on him. His T-shirt was wet with sweat, and was stuck to his back, and I could almost see the muscles as they moved and shifted under the fabric. I lifted my chin. "And I kept all the mess right there on the tarp. See?"

He lifted one tarp with the toe of his work boot, noticed the second, and squatted to take a closer look.

"Two? This isn't exactly battery acid here."

I squatted down beside him. "I'm not taking any chances with my floor."

"Your floor is just plywood."

"It's still a lot more than when I first got here."

He stared a minute, then stood, laughing. "That's right. You're first walk-through was a little rough."

I stood next to him. "Looking better now, though. In fact, I think I'm going to like if here."

He looked around. "Anything I can do for you right now?"

You could tell me what a wonderful job I did stripping off that old paint. You could compliment me on looking cool and sexy in this blistering heat, even though there was sweat dripping off my nose and my shirt was sticking under my boobs. You could mention what a great time you had on Saturday, and how you couldn't wait to spend some *more* time with me.

I shook my head. "No, I got this. I'm going to do the drawers, next. I'll probably have to pry the handles off with some tool I'll need to borrow from Tyler."

"A crowbar?" Mike suggested.

"No, I don't think I need to go that big. I think I'll be fine until I have to do the inside here. These shelves are not what I want, they're not *where* I want them, and they'll be a pain to paint around."

Mike looked and nodded. "Welp. I'll have a word with one of the boys here, and we'll just cut them out with the SawzAll, give you a nice, big, empty box. How 'bout that?"

"That sounds great."

"I gotta say, Chris. You're doing okay with this."

I felt my heart start to swell. My cheeks, I knew, were flaming. Should I just bat my lashes modestly? Smile sheepishly?

Before I could formulate a suitable reply, preferably cute and possibly suggestive, a woman came through my front door. She was, quite possibly, the most beautiful woman I'd ever seen in real life. She was tall and slender, but with just the right amount of boob and hip to create quite the silhouette. Her skin was clear, her hair sleek and dark in a short bob, and her eyes were bright blue.

"You Politтano?" she asked.

I nodded.

Behind me, I could feel the entire room shrink back. From the corner of my eye, I saw Tyler duck into a doorway. The sounds of nailing ceased, quite abruptly Joe made a noise, something between a snarl and a whimper.

Mike cleared his throat. "Well hello Amy. Good to see you, too."

Amy McCann was wearing a bodycon dress and heels so high and pointed they could have been used as a murder weapon. She took a few more steps into the house and looked around.

"This one of yours, Mike?" she asked.

He cleared his throat. "Yep. And you know about that other job of mine across the street?"

She focused on me, taking in my sweaty clothes and the brushes and containers on the floor around me. "What on earth are you doing?"

"Stripping," I said calmly, peeling off my canvas gloves, and then the latex gloves I was wearing underneath.

She glared at Mike. "And what are you doing?"

Mike grinned. "Watching her strip."

It unsettled her, I could tell. She frowned, and I could practically see her reformulating her approach. "I just got off the phone with Celeste Montecorvo," she said in a neutral tone.

I dropped all my gloves on the tarp. "And how is she?"

"She's just fine. But she told me that she's still thinking about the very fair offer I made on her property a week ago, and when I asked her why she was taking so long, she told me I should talk to you. Now, why on earth would you have anything to say about this?" Amy's voice was completely reasonable, as was her question, but I could see the impatience and irritation in her eyes. I smiled, because I knew exactly what to do with her.

In the course of being a realtor, I'd encountered pretty much every different type of person that existed, and I immediately knew what type she was. She was the customer who couldn't understand why her puny budget couldn't buy her a brand new condo with three bathrooms. She was the customer who'd get angry if I didn't answer her phone calls at eleven o'clock at night. She was the customer who, three days before closing, came up with a to-do list for the seller, usually involving expensive cosmetic work, and didn't understand I wouldn't do anything with it except tear it up.

The thing is I still managed to sell houses to even those types of customers. I knew what they were like, what they really wanted, and better yet, how to deflect their feeling of entitlement.

I hadn't been in my realtor mode for weeks now, but I slid right in with no effort at all. "Well, you see, Amy—may I call you Amy? You see, Celeste was saying how she hated to think about all those lovely trees of hers getting cut down, and you know how she loves those ducks. Then we started talking about her garden, and her vines...did you know she had grapevines back there? And one thing led to another, and what else could I do but suggest that maybe, just maybe, I knew someone who might have a different vision for her land. She was so grateful, I mean, *really* grateful. She was torn, because, well, because of you. She told me what a shrewd businesswoman you were. And she told me how you hated to be disappointed. But honestly, what could I do? The poor woman was practically in tears." I shrugged my shoulders. "It's nothing personal."

"If you're interfering with my business," she said slowly, "it's very personal."

I shook my head. "Oh, Amy, come on. A woman like you? I bet you have a dozen projects just waiting for your attention. The Coop? Small potatoes I'm sure."

Her eyes narrowed. "All of my projects are of equal importance."

"I'm sure they are. But let me tell you, Amy." I took a step forward and lowered my voice, just us girls. "I haven't had a chance to speak to my friend just yet, and I know for a fact he's in the middle of something else right now, so this may come to nothing at all. But I had to tell Celeste something, right? I'm sure you understand. The last thing you want to deal with in any negotiation is a person who thinks they could get something better from somewhere else." I dropped my voice again. "So, maybe just ride this out for another week? See if anything plays out?"

Her lips drew out into a thin line, and she glanced over my shoulder.

"You're looking pretty good, Mike," she said.

"Yeah, well, eating healthy, not drinking to much, you know...just trying to do the right thing."

"You don't know anything about this friend of hers, do you?"

My irritation kicked up a notch. "Amy. I'm right here."

Her eyes flickered to me, and then back to Mike. "Mike?"

"Why, Amy, I have no idea what you're getting out. Chris here is my client. I'm just here to build her house." His voice was pitched a bit higher than normal, but other than that, he sounded just fine.

I was thinking about maybe throwing a bit of paint stripper in her direction to remind her I was standing *right there*.

"I didn't appreciate that SOB from Rehoboth coming in here and stealing my retail center," she said.

"Welp, now, Amy, I don't think that stealing is quite the truth here. He just moved a little faster than you did."

"Yeah. Friggin' ninja."

"Amy," I said, very loudly. "We were talking about Celeste."

She brought her eyes back to me. "Of course. And you're right. I don't want Celeste upset and worried about this deal. I want her to feel perfectly comfortable. I can afford a few more days." She shrugged her shoulders and swept her hair back with perfectly manicured fingers. "But Mike here can tell you, I don't like to lose." She turned and walked out, quickly, her heels echoing sharply against my plywood floor.

Mike moved behind me and we watched her as she crossed the street and climb into a convertible Mercedes parked at the curb. He let out a low whistle.

"You must have been one hell of a realtor," he said.

I nodded slowly. "I sure was. When is Daniel coming back?"

"Should be here now. He sent me a text. He's staying right in town. Got a month-long rental, over the wine and cheese shop, he said." He nudged me, and I could hear the laughter in his voice. "Isn't that where you're staying with Terri?"

I dropped my chin to my chest and nodded.

"Well, that's convenient. He said third floor rear. You could run up there right now and make your pitch."

I turned slowly and glared at him. "You're enjoying this, aren't you."

He chuckled. "I've never seen anyone handle Amy like that. Ever. It was better than the movies."

"Next time," I said, "I'll charge admission."

"And next time, I'll pay."

I walked down to the wine and cheese shop, entered the door on the side, walked up past Terri's apartment and on up to the third floor.

There were eight units in the building, four on each floor, two front, overlooking Main Street, and two overlooking the rear alley. I stopped on the third-floor landing and looked at the two doors the led to the rear units. I took breath and knocked on both.

The door on the left opened, and Daniel stood there, frowning.

"Did you fly up? Isn't there supposed to be a bell or something to let people in?"

I pushed past him. "I know the code, because I'm staying with Terri. One floor down."

His eyebrows shot up and I laughed.

"Right? I'm just starting to appreciate small-town living."

His place was basically the same layout as Terri's but furnished more along the lines of a very nice hotel. Everything was neutral, the art on the walls generic, the furniture simple.

He had already set up an office space on the dining room table: two laptops, a printer, and portable file boxes.

"Well, do come in," he said, closing the door behind me. "What on earth have you been doing? You're a mess. You smell of paint stripper, and there appears to be something a cat may have coughed up on your shoe."

"I was stripping old paint off of an armoire. I do things like that now."

"Oh, my. Is that good?'" We went into his living room. "Drink? It's a bit early, and I know you really don't drink all that much, but as my first official guest?"

"What have you got?" I asked, settling into a corner of his couch.

"Sadly, only tequila and bourbon."

"Tequila. Please."

He raised both eyebrows, but a few minutes later bought over two shot glasses, a bottle of Don Patron, lemons and a small saucer of salt.

We silently clicked out glasses, and I licked the salt off my thumb, took the shot, and sucked on the lemon slice.

"Well," he said. "You did that rather well."

"Two years ago, when I was here," I told him, "I got drunk on tequila shots and went skinny-dipping in the bay."

His eyes widened. "But you never get drunk," he whispered.

I nodded. "I know."

"And you didn't even like for *me* to see you naked."

"I *know*. It's this place, I think. Or maybe what this place represents."

"Which is?" he asked. He was like that, intensely curious about everything. That was one of the reasons I fell for him. When he talked to me, he made me feel that he was listening to every word and that what I said was important to his personal happiness. It was a powerful feeling, and because of it, I overlooked a lot of his other, not as attractive, traits.

But the last thing I wanted now was a philosophical discussion. "I'm here because I have a business proposal for you."

He settled back and clasped his fingers together. "Do go on."

"There's a piece of property about eight or nine miles up Rt. 31. A building that's probably not worth two cents, but lots of acreage and highway frontage. It would be perfect for your village idea. In fact, you could call it, The Village in Northampton."

"Northampton being the county, I assume?" He nodded. "How interesting. Why, exactly, would I want to do this again?"

"Because you've been talking about this idea for as long as I've known you, but you could never find a parcel with enough land in the right place at the right time. The stars have aligned, Daniel. Your moment is here."

"Ah, Yes. Okay, now tell me the real reason?"

I held out my shot glass. He refilled it, and his, and we took another shot.

"The property is owned by two little Italian women, and—"

"Wait. Are these the same two women who think you all came from some pinprick on the map of Italy?"

"Yes. Anyway, Connie is in a nursing home, and Celeste wants to get her out and move somewhere else and finally retire, but to do that they need lots of money, so they're selling." I leaned forward. "Here's the thing, Daniel. There's enough land that you could build your little village, hell, maybe two, and still have lots of trees left, and there's a pond way out in the woods with ducks, so you could have some land as a reserve. It would be a perfect mix of commercial and residential, and at the same time, all the locals will love you for not tearing down all the trees and not displacing all those ducks." The tequila was kicking in. "You wouldn't want to displace ducks now, would you?"

His eyes got very narrow. "It's quite ways from the beach."

"Exactly. But you wanted studio and loft space, right? Affordable housing is really in demand here. You could easily sell to singles and Millennials. You wouldn't have to depend on folks investing to cater to the tourists."

"The problem is, if retail space goes in there, all your trees and ducks would have to go for parking."

"But...the reason I want you to do this in the first place is to save the trees and ducks. How about...professional space? Offices?"

He sat up abruptly. "The MedCenter," he said.

"What about it?"

"They're breaking ground for phase two in the spring. And that means more doctors, and all those doctors will need office space, and then they'll need space for labs and rehab centers, and drug treatment centers, and sleep centers...a medical park."

"Medical park?"

"Oh, my God. I'm brilliant. A medical park. Doctors love trees and things. I could put in a walking path and one of those fitness trails, where you walk a few hundred feet then do some sort of exercise...that would leave plenty of trees. And there can still be residential units, and because doctors don't have hours at night there won't be a need for parking for patients, and employees *and* residents...it's perfect." He looked at me, his eyes bright. "Absolutely perfect."

"And much better than what Amy probably had planned."

He held up a hand. "Amy who?"

"Amy McCann. She wants the property too, but I convinced Celeste to put her off until you had a chance to look around and see if it was what you've been looking for."

"This Amy person has a rather nasty reputation."

"So?"

"And apparently, she's already got it in for me about the Main Street project."

"Again, so? What is she going to do? Trash you on Twitter?" I leaned forward. "You said you wanted a foot in the door. This could be it, Daniel."

He shook his head. "There are too many unknowns, here, Chris. Why would I—"

"I know a property lawyer who can give you all the scoop." I held out my glass and waggled it. "Another shot and I'd probably give up her number."

He unclasped his hands and reached for his phone. "Give me the number first. Another shot and you might forget her name."

"It's Marie Wu." I pulled my phone out of my purse and read off Marie's number.

Daniel dialed and spoke. "Daniel Russo calling for Marie Wu. Is she available? Tell her it's about, ah, Chris Polittano's land grab deal."

Marie must have taken the call, because Daniel abruptly stood and walked outside to the large deck that opened out off the living room. Spending time with Daniel felt so comfortable, and I remembered how often we'd spend hours just talking. But he'd never, not even in the beginnings of our relationship, made my heart pound the way it did when I was around Mike.

I closed my eyes and let the hot air coming in from the open sliding glass wash over me. I think I may have dozed for just a few minutes before Daniel spoke my name.

"Christiana? My God, have you passed out?"

I sat up. "No. What did Marie say?"

"Quite a lot. She's obviously one of those frighteningly intelligent people who not only have their facts straight, but can speak in brief, succinct sentences. I may be in love."

"Oh?" One thing about Daniel was his ability to shift alliances at the drop of a hat. "What about Chloe?"

He shot me a look. "I was lonely after you left, and Chloe, well, she just suddenly appeared and started doing everything for me, and being everywhere, and she finally told me she was in love with me. What was I supposed to do?"

"Think with your brain instead of your—

"Don't be nasty. You never did like her." He sat down across from me, arms crossed. "This Marie person said I could probably get approval from the county for anything I wanted as long as I came up with the right bottom line for them, tax-wise."

I was silent. Daniel thought out loud. Mostly because he liked the sound of his own voice, but he insisted it helped him think to hear the ideas floating out in the air.

"She also suggested that the sisters would knock a million off the price if I promised to save their ducks. I thought they needed the money?"

"They do, but all they want is enough to live comfortably for the rest of their lives. And they're pretty old. It's not like they want a yacht or a trip around the world."

"According to Ms. Wu, for what that property is worth, they could go around the world a few times."

"But they'd rather know that the ducks are safe."

He sighed. "I don't suppose it would hurt to talk to them."

"You could go tomorrow," I said. "First thing."

"I suppose..."

"But don't wear one of your expensive suits. Go in jeans. Or shorts. And maybe a baseball cap."

He snorted. "You know I don't own a baseball cap. Okay, I will. But just to look the place over, Chris. Don't start spreading the word around this little one-horse burg that I'm even interested. Understand?"

"My lips are sealed," I said. "Your secret is safe with me."

He rolled his eyes. "And for God's sakes, swear Terri and all your friends to secrecy as well, because I bet you've already talked to half of them about this already."

I rose with dignity. "That's an unfair accusation, Daniel, but I'll forgive you."

We walked to his front door and he gave me a cool kiss on the cheek. "Just a friendly heads up," he murmured in my ear, "that both of the McCann brothers have asked me about you."

I felt my cheeks start to burn. "Oh?"

"Is this new life you're living turning into something a bit...*frisky*? I mean, two brothers..."

I pushed him back into his apartment, pulled the front door shut, and went downstairs.

Terri looked up as I came through her door, phone in hand. She handed it to me. "The timing is amazing. It's Marie," she said.

I stared at her phone, then held it to my ear.

"Chris? Did you put your phone on mute? I've been calling," Marie said briskly. "I spoke to Daniel."

"Yes, I know. I was there. Well, when he dialed, at least. I didn't hear the conversation, but whatever you told him convinced him to go out there tomorrow and talk to Celeste."

"Excellent. Talking to him was a hoot. He sounds like a character in one of those British detective shows."

I grinned. "I know. All he needs is the accent. He seemed interested."

"Good. Amy is a bitch, and I'd love to see her fall."

"I met her, by the way."

Terri, who had been puttering in the kitchen, appeared in a flash, eyes wide open.

"You what?" Marie asked. "Met Amy? Where?"

"She came to the house this afternoon. Apparently, Celeste put her off again. I told Celeste that if Amy gave her a hard time to just send her to me, and, well...she did. So Amy showed up, guns drawn."

Terri's mouth dropped open and she let out a tiny squeal.

"What did she say? And what did *you* say?" Marie asked.

"Amy wanted to know why I was involved in the first place, so I gave her what my partners used to call the bait and switch. I did it all the time with entitled clients who felt like they were better than all those silly rules. Convince the client that what you're doing is in their absolute best interest, even make it seem like it's their idea, then do the right thing anyway. Usually by the time the client realized they weren't going to get their way after all, they were at closing, and if they backed out they'd look like complete jerks. Its amazing what people will do to avoid looking stupid in front of others."

She laughed. "I wish I'd been there. Okay, just wanted to check back. Talk soon." She hung up and I did too, handing the phone back to Terri and looking for my own. Sure enough, when I'd looked for her number earlier I hit must have hit Mute.

"Why didn't you tell me about Amy?" Terri said.

"Terri, I had just walked through the door..."

"What else didn't you tell me?'

"Daniel is going to look at that property. He may buy it."

"I gathered that. Tell me something I didn't overhear?"

"Have I talked to you lately about Mike?"

"What?" Another squeal. "No! What about Mike?"

"He believes that I have no interest in dating anyone right now. In theory, that would include him."

"Now, Chris, honey...how would he get a stupid idea like that?"

"Because while we were having our lovely coffee and conversation last week, I *told* him I wasn't interested in dating anyone right now, that's how. It's what I said to Steve and we were talking about Steve, and about how he'd asked me out, and I said no...I couldn't lie. I mean, they're brothers. At some point they'd probably compare notes."

"Well...poop. But you were out with him all day Saturday. Didn't anything happen?"

"No, because for all my talk about taking chances and being bold, when push came to shove, I couldn't kiss him when I really *really* wanted to. I'm a total chicken."

"Oh, honey." She sat beside me and leaned her head against my shoulder. "What are you going to do?"

"No clue." I sighed. I meant it. Unless Steve got sidetracked..."Next week you're on vacation, right?"

She nodded. "I'm going to grout."

"Oh?"

"Yes. I called Steve, and told him that I was planning to spend the whole week helping out, and he said I would be there while they were grouting the bathroom. I'm pretty excited."

"You know I'm not going to be there, right? I have to go back to Rehoboth on Sunday. Mom's house. The walkthrough is Monday, I close on Tuesday, and Wednesday I meet with Patty and Sara to close out the business." My partners and I had finally reached an agreement months before, but the paperwork had yet to be signed.

"I know. I'll miss you, but I have my own work cut out for me."

"Terri, don't try too hard with Steve."

"What do you mean?"

"Women in this town have been falling all over him for years. And not one of them has stuck. Doesn't that tell you something?"

"Yes. He hasn't met the right woman."

I sighed. "No. What—"

"Was she pretty?" Terri asked.

"Amy McCann? Oh yeah. Stunning. With a body that didn't quit."

Unlike mine, with those little saggy spots, and the soft little pooch around the belly, not to mention short legs and hair with a mind of its own.

"How old, do you think?"

"Late thirties."

"And she's supposed to be *quite* the sharp mind."

"So I hear."

She leaned her head against mine again. "But she's no Chris Polittano."

I smiled. "No. She certainly is not."

Chapter Eight

I walked to the house the next morning and found Judd sitting on the porch steps. He waved as I came up the sidewalk.

"I just had a marvelous conversation with your neighbor, Miss Ava. She's kind of a celebrity around here, did you know?"

I shook my head. "No, I didn't know."

"She's actually *Dr.* Wilson, and she's a very well-known and well-respected conservationist. She's still an advisor to the State Wildlife Division, and she's testified in front of Congress."

I grinned in surprise. "And here I thought she was just a good gardener."

He grinned. "She's that too. Her roses are just beautiful."

"Yes. I'm thinking of asking her for advice if I ever decide to do something with is front yard besides grass and one azalea."

He waved a hand. "You've got plenty of time. You've made lots of progress inside," he said. "I'd like another series of pictures. Things are really looking up!"

The crew was there, of course, including Steve, and a dour-looking man with an iPad.

"Inspections," Steve explained briefly. "We should get electrical cleared, and HVAC."

"Does that mean I can turn on the air-conditioning?" I asked.

Steve flashed killer grin. "Not yet. You really should wait for the *final* inspection."

"Can Judd take pictures?"

Steve nodded. "Snap away." He and the inspector walked around to the back of the house, and Judd and I went through the front door.

Judd took lots of pictures, admired my purchases, and even took a few shots of my armoire.

"This is very nice," Judd said. "Where is it going?"

I explained, and even showed him the newly reframed opening in the hall where it would soon be going.

He frowned. "So, it's sliding in here?"

I nodded.

"So, basically, except for the door and drawers, the rest of this will be, well, hidden?"

I looked. I had spent a great deal of time and energy on...the outside of the armoire. The part that would be behind framing and drywall. The part that no one would see. I sighed. "Well, I guess it was good practice for my great idea."

He laughed. "It's going to look very cool, Chris. I promise. In fact, I'll make sure to give you a shout-out. 'The homeowner repurposed an old kitchen cabinet into functional storage.'"

"It's an *armoire*," I corrected. I heard voices, and Steve and the inspector, as well as Alan, came in through the side door. Judd and I slipped out the front, settled ourselves on the porch, and alternately watched what was going on across the street and tried to hear what was going on inside my house.

"There are a lot more workers over there," Judd observed.

"Yes. But it is two stories and four units long. Daniel has a much larger budget." Mike popped his head out of an upstairs window, waved, then appeared a few minutes later, darted across the street, and bounded up the steps, Joe at his heels.

"Inspection day, right?"

I nodded. He sat right next to me on the step, and my body temperature shot up by at least five degrees. He leaned toward me, and our shoulders touched. "Not to worry. It's all good," he whispered.

He smelled of sawdust and sweat, and something else, faint and musky. I wanted to stick my face into his chest and just breathe in.

"How are the pictures coming?" he asked Judd.

Judd kept his face neutral. "Getting lots of good ones." He lifted his camera and snapped at Mike and I, sitting close, my face probably the same shade as a red maple leaf, Mike grinning.

"Save that one," Mike said. "It'll be worth money some day. Right Chris?"

"Right," I croaked. Mike's forearms were resting on his knees, his strong hands clasped together, and I could see the muscles move beneath his skin, and saw where a vein was throbbing...

I stood up. "Gotta stretch," I mumbled, and hopped down a few steps.

Joe suddenly took off and bounded into the empty lot next door and reared up against one of the trees.

"Looks like he found something interesting," Judd said.

Mike made a face. "Probably another damn squirrel. He never catches them, but he keeps trying." He whistled sharply between his teeth, and Joe abandoned his effort and returned to the porch.

"Daniel went over to see Celeste," Mike said. "Left a few minutes ago. I suggested he take her out to lunch."

"Good plan," I said. I turned and balanced on my toes, then dropped down. Up on toes, and...down.

"Don't be nervous," Mike said. "I told you, it's all good."

I caught Judd's eye and saw him choke back a laugh. He knew that whatever was making me nervous had nothing at all to do with the inspection going on inside the house, but rather what was going on right there on the front porch.

"This is the first I've seen Joe for a while," I said, desperate for any normal conversation.

Mike sat back, resting his elbows on the step behind and stretching his legs out in front of him. "Joe doesn't like the noise," he said. "It's too loud for him across the street."

"He could hang with me," I offered. "Maybe take another crack at the super-squirrel?"

Mike grinned. "The what?"

I nodded in the direction of the vacant lot. "My neighbor tells me I've got a rare and talented squirrel living somewhere over there. I saw her once, and she's twice the size of your average squirrel, so Joe better watch out. She might fight back. Name's Bella. She's a Delmarva fox squirrel, and she's endangered. If Joe does catch her, he could do hard time."

Mike made a face. "I used to shoot them out of trees for fun when I was kid. Course, I got my butt whipped for it, and when I finally grew a brain I realized how awful it was. Poor things, just trying to gather a few nuts." His cotton button-down shirt was stretched across his chest and I could see his shoulders straining against the fabric. "But Joe would probably like spending the day with you," Mike said. His eyes met mine, twinkling. "You wouldn't mind me running over here just to check up on him, would you?"

I shook my head. Up on my toes, down. Up, down. "Nope. Not at all."

Steve called Mike's name, and Mike got up and went through the front door. Joe got up and went back to the vacant lot and sat under the same tree, looking up hopefully.

Judd shook his head at me, his eyes brimming with laughter. "You lied to me girlfriend. You told me you weren't interested in the McCann brothers."

"And I'm not. Interested in the brothers, I mean. Just *one* brother."

"Have you got it bad or what?" he said

"Quiet," I hissed. "And no I don't. I mean, yes. Very bad."

"You turned six different shades of red when he sat down. Is the man blind?"

I sat back down. "No. He just has very good reason to think I have no interest in him at all. And until I gather up enough nerve to break the news to him, he will continue to think that way."

Mike, Steve and Alan all came out on the porch, followed by the inspector, who nodded to us all and went past and down the sidewalk.

"Well?" I asked.

Alan shook his head. "Oh ye of little faith."

Mike reached out and squeezed my shoulder. "Everything went fine. All gold stars. I told you we had this."

Our eyes met and his hand on my shoulder felt like lead. No, not lead. It was a magnet, drawing me in, bringing me closer and I swear I could see his mouth starting to form a smile, and his expression softened just a bit and I was almost ready to stand back up on my toes so I could better reach those lips...

Steve clapped his hands together. "Maybe we should celebrate? Lunch down at Sam's on Main?"

Mike's hand slipped off my shoulder and I dropped my eyes. Did I really almost kiss him in front of Steve and Alan and God and everybody?

"Thanks bro," Mike said. "But one of us has a job site to manage. But enjoy yourselves." He glanced at me again, and I smiled brightly.

"How about it, Chris?" Steve asked easily.

Damn. "Ah, Sorry. Can't," I said. "Judd and I just made a date. Curtains. I need to buy, ah, curtains..."

"And I told her I'd drive her across the Bay Bridge," Judd said smoothly. "A lot more choices across the bay."

"Yes, that there are," Mike agreed, quite heartily. "Happy shopping."

"Thanks. Yes, I love shopping."

Steve shrugged. "Alan, how about you and me, then?"

Alan had been watching Mike and I, and he shook his head, as though to chase off a gnat. "Yeah, sure. Why not?"

I stood and watched as Mike whistled for Joe, and the three men walked off.

Judd exploded in a choked laugh. "Even Alan saw it. What is wrong with those two brothers anyway?"

I sighed. "I have no idea, but they're both driving me crazy."

"Are we really buying curtains?"

"I need to. Would you mind? I'll go by myself, but..."

He waved a hand. "No worries. I'll even drive. Now?"

I shook my head. "Not quite. I have to go in the house and measure every damn window, and I don't have a tape measure, which means I have to ask Tyler, and he's going make a big production out of it...maybe I can just staple some sheets over my windows and call it a day?"

He shuddered. "Don't you dare. Come on, let's measure."

I looked at him. "You're a good friend. Thank you."

He laughed. "Thanks. It's easy. You're just so entertaining."

So we went shopping.

Judd drove north after crossing the bridge. "There are a dozen malls and shopping centers up this way," he told me. "Are we going Luxe or budget?"

"Budget. I still don't have a job."

We managed to find curtains, drapes, sheers, valances, curtain rods, those fancy things at the ends of the curtain rods...

"I had no idea this was going to be so complicated," I muttered when we finally sat down at a small restaurant for very late lunch. "This owning a house thing is pretty involved. And this was just about *curtains*."

"You sound like this is your first house," he said.

"It is. I mean, it's the first house that's just mine. Not my parents' or my husband's or my boyfriend's. This is mine, and I feel like I'm finally all grown up." I shook my head. "I've been telling clients all through the years about the joy of owning their own home, about how much fun it would be, and how rewarding...I feel like I owe them all an apology. This is so much friggin' work."

He sat back, looking relaxed and dapper. "At least you'll know that pretty much your entire home will be brand new, so you won't have leaking roof issues or crumbling foundation problems or electrical problems, plumbing problems—"

I held up a hand. "Please, Stop. I can't even think about dealing with any of *that*. How do people do it? Building a house? It's torture!"

He smiled. "Don't think of it as building a *house*. Think of it as building...home. Then you'll look at things differently."

I stared at the menu. "You're right. Building home. I do like that better. And that's what I'm doing. It's part of a whole new life, one where it's just about me. This is the first time in my life I'll be living somewhere without having to think about some other person being there too. I can do what I want, when I want, and never have to ask or explain to anyone. It feels amazing."

"And where does Mike McCann fit into all this?"

I sighed. I put down the menu. "I'm not sure. I did not move to Cape Edwards to find a new man, although Terri did dangle that in front of me as part of the bait to get me down here in the first place. Mike is...something very new for me. He's a very interesting combination of things. He left high finance for construction, and he not only made a success in a tough field, he seems to love it. He's got this good-ole-boy persona, but he's really sharp. And he's a desirable bachelor in a community of single women who would gobble him right up, but he's managed to stay detached."

"Until now?" Judd asked. The waitress took our orders and I looked out the window, watching the passersby.

"Maybe." I looked at him. "I don't think it's just me. I think he's got a few...feelings, but he's not acting on them because Steve asked me out first."

"Oh. Yeah, that could be a problem."

"And when I turned Steve down, I told him that I just didn't want any kind of relationship right now. And then, I had to tell the same thing to *Mike*, and now..."

He whistled between his teeth. "You have totally screwed yourself over, haven't you?"

I sighed. "Yes. I don't know what's more exhausting, the house or figuring out what to do with Mike and Steve." I looked at him. "What about you? How's your love life?"

He smiled crookedly. "I'm a gay man in a small southern town. Folks don't mind my being gay, understand, because I look just like any average bald guy."

"Actually, Judd, you're much more attractive than the average bald guy."

He flashed a smile. "Well thank you, I think so too."

"But?"

"But nothing. I had a very serious relationship that ended about two years ago. I'm not interested in casual sex. I also believe that there's a plan for my life, and if I'm meant to be with someone, it will happen. In the meantime, I'm not going to cruise gay bars. So I take pictures, enjoy my friends, and live vicariously through the complicated love lives of the fair citizens of Cape Edwards. And believe me, that's exciting enough."

I rolled my eyes. "Well, at least I'm keeping you entertained."

We ate for a while in companionable silence.

"So what are you doing about a job?" he asked.

I sighed and sipped my seltzer. "It's not an immediate concern, but I can't spend all my time sitting on my porch watching tourists on Main Street."

"True. Especially since they'll be all gone by September, and then you'll be really bored. Try the MedCenter."

"I don't know anything about medical billing or insurance."

He shook his head. "It's not that kind of a job. I think they're looking for an office manager."

"I could do that. Wow. My own house, and a job...just like a real grown-up."

He grinned and reached over to clink his glass against mine. "Happy adulthood."

"Amen to that, my friend."

On the way home I got a text from Marie, suggesting I meet her for Buck A Beer night at DeeDee and Jacks. I texted back a quick yes.

"Wanna come with?" I asked Judd as we turned north off the Bay Bridge.

He shook his head. "No, thanks. But I'll drop you. I'm sure you can get a ride back."

A second text pinged a few minutes later, this time from Daniel.

Just escaped Celeste God help me I need a drink where is the nearest bar????

Where ru?

RT31 heading south

Stop just before the Methodist church and go into the building on left that looks condemned with all the cars out front. Meet u there in ten

I grinned. "Daniel just now left Celeste. I'm directing him to DeeDee and Jacks."

Judd laughed. "Didn't Mike say he went over there this morning?"

"Yep. Poor Daniel. I bet she fed him."

He dropped me in front of DeeDee and Jacks. It was the kind of place the tourists drove past because they couldn't imagine why anyone would voluntarily go in. The outside looked like a deserted airplane hangar. The inside wasn't too many steps up from that, but the crowd was friendly and the food delicious.

Tuesday drew a big crowd, but when I walked in I saw that Marie had snagged a corner booth and was sitting across from Karen and Stella. I went over and slid in.

"Daniel is meeting me. He is in need of a drink."

"I've been filling the ladies on the situation," Marie said. "He texted me all day, a barrage of legal questions about zoning and variances and designated green space. Celeste must have given him quite a tour."

"What a coincidence, his being just across the street like that," Stella said, eyebrows raised.

"And working so closely with Mike," Karen added, throwing me a grin.

I shook my head. "Ladies, you can dream all you want, but there's no drama here. Daniel is a charming and lovely man. He is also something of a pompous ass. But above all, he is someone I am *over.* There's no secret longing left, no *gee, I wish* moments." I slapped my palms down on the tabletop. "I am done."

I looked up as the door slammed open, and Daniel stood, looking completely haggard and slightly wild-eyed. He saw me and closed his eyes, put his hands together in silent prayer, and came over.

Stella scooched in to give him more room on her side of the booth. He sat gratefully and put his head down on the tabletop.

I nudged him under the table with my foot. "Manners, Daniel. This Karen Helfman and Stella Blount, and you've kind of already met Marie here."

He lifted his head and nodded. "It's a pleasure. Sincerely. Especially after..." He lowered his voice. "That woman."

DeeDee hurried over. Daniel followed my advice and did not wear a suit, but in his expensive jeans, hand-tailored shirt and Italian shoes, he did not look like a regular.

"Welcome," she said brightly. "What can I get you?"

He lifted his head. "Oh, thank God you're here. A martini, please. Stoli Elit. Very *very* dry. With a twist."

Her smile remained fixed. "Stoli what?"

"Elit," he repeated slowly.

"We really don't do that here," DeeDee explained patiently.

"Vodka rocks," I told her. "With lime. And I'll have a beer. Bud."

He scowled at me. "Since when do you drink beer?" he grumbled. "And who doesn't have Stoli Elit?"

He could be such a spoiled baby sometimes. If we had still been together, I would have tried to charm or joke away his mood. But now, I was just trying not to laugh. "Daniel, be nice," I scolded.

He put his hand to his chest, fingers splayed. "I'm always nice." His eyes lit up. "Marie, I cannot begin to express my thanks. Your information was invaluable today. As was your subtle wit and words of advice. Thanks to you, was able to keep up with that woman..."

"Who is a dear," I said.

He was still looking at Marie. "Who is sly as a fox and would have happily eaten me alive if not for Marie here."

I glanced at Marie. Her eyes were bright and she was looking very smug.

"So I gather you two had lots to talk about?" I prompted.

"She showed me *everything*. I had to walk miles into those woods because she insisted I see the pond, which is almost a lake, by the way, and the ducks swarmed us, because, apparently, she feeds them and they must have been starving because I barely got out alive."

DeeDee appeared with the drinks. Daniel drank his at once in a long gulp, closed his eyes and winced.

"Another," he croaked.

Off she went.

"And then we saw her garden. And then the grape arbor. There's also a small shed back in there somewhere with everything you could ever need to make your own wine." He clasped his hands together. "A small meth lab in the corner would not have surprised me. And then she suggested lunch, and I thought, finally, we can go somewhere and talk like two business people, but no." He shook his head. "She had something prepared. Actually, she had about ten different somethings prepared. So we sat in her kitchen and we ate for hours and she tried to kill me with glass of her wine, which luckily I nursed throughout the meal or I would have been flat on the floor."

Another drink arrived, and this time he sipped it. "She loved my ideas and wanted me to draw the plans for her, right there. She had paper and a red pencil. Very quaint. So I drew a very rough sketch, then she started changing things, then she forced more wine down my throat, and then she dragged me back outside so we could pace it off. Pace. It. Off. In ninety-degree heat, and the humidity is what, seven hundred percent? And after eating that tremendous meal and drinking that lethal concoction of hers, which I imagine has an alcoholic equivalency of *grain*, I felt sure I was going to pass out. The only thing that kept me upright was the fear that if I did collapse, she'd leave me there and I'd be eaten by something. Probably a bear. Or maybe a flock of ravenous ducks."

At this point, Stella and Karen were trying so hard not to laugh that I was afraid they were going to each burst a blood vessel. Marie's mouth was a thin line, but I could feel her body next to mine, shaking with suppressed laughter.

"She asked me what part of Italy my family was from," Daniel continued. He leaned toward Marie and dropped his voice. "My family were Russian Jews who came here and changed their name from Russokov. I was afraid to tell her, so I just said Rome. That worked for some reason. And then, just to make the entire afternoon *completely* absurd, she said that if I built an assisted living facility back near her duck pond, and made sure she and her sister could live there for free, she'd give me back half the money. Half." He shuddered. "She's diabolical."

"That sounds like an amazing deal, Daniel," I said, and I meant it. "So, what did you think?"

"I think that the sooner she's put into protective custody, the safer this entire state will be."

"Daniel," I said, trying to keep my voice from cracking. "She's a sweet lady who was trying to make you feel welcome."

He stared into his drink. "Yes, well...that stuff she ferments out there and puts into those bottles needs a *very* strong warning label," he muttered. "I barely sobered up enough to realize how badly I needed a *real* drink. And then to come here, where they don't even have *Stoli Elit...*"

"You asked me lots of questions today, Daniel," Marie said, her shaking under control. "Did you form any opinion?"

He slowly drank a bit more and nodded. "Yes. The property is ideal for what I'd like, and there's more than enough acreage for some sort of old-person's home tucked back there. I've never actually done a project quite like that, but if she's going to give me back half the money just so she can feed her ducks every day...whole thing is very doable. Marie, if I can get the zoning changed as easily as you seem to think I can, I can buy in a few weeks, and start construction early next year."

Karen clapped her hands. "Daniel, you're a hero."

"No, I'm not," he said. "I do not do this sort of thing just to rescue wildlife, or any other kind of life. I do it to make money, and with this deal I'm going to make lots of it. That is why I do this"

I grabbed his hand and kissed it. If he pulled this off, in a few years Celeste and Connie were going to be right back where they belonged. "And think of all those ducks you saved," I said, finally laughing out loud.

He glared at me. "This Amy person had better not cause any trouble, Chris. I mean it. I do not need my reputation besmirched."

Marie cackled. "Besmirched? Really? You use words like that all the time?"

He looked at her, and I saw something in his eyes. "As a matter of fact," he said slowly. "I do. I'm quite an admirer of the English language and like to express my appreciation as often as possible."

Marie pointed her index finger at him. "Really? And here thought you liked the sound of your own voice."

Daniel's eyes glittered. "And is there anything *wrong* with the sound of my voice?"

A funny look passed over her face. "No. There's not."

He looked back down at his drink, nodded, as though to himself, and downed it quickly. "I probably can't drive myself back to town," he said, to no one in particular.

Marie straightened her shoulders. "I'll be happy to drive you back."

A slow, satisfied smile crossed his face. "Why, thank you. That's very kind."

I slid out so she could go, and stayed standing as I watched the two of them leave. He held the door open for her, and as he went to close it behind him, he flashed me a very wicked grin.

I sat down.

"Did what I think happened," Karen said slowly, "just happen?"

I stared into my beer. "Yes, I think so. I think that Daniel and Marie are going back to his place, have another drink or two, and then proceed to have some terrifically hot sex."

Karen swore softly. "But they just met."

"But they've been texting back and forth all day," I said.

"Texting?" Stella said. "Does that even count as anything?"

"As someone who's read many of Daniel's texts, yes, they can count for quite a lot. He can be quite charming."

Stella sighed. "A casual meeting, a few melting looks across the table and, bingo! Instant attraction. I didn't think that sort of thing happened in real life."

"Well it's happening to Chris here," Karen said. "She just doesn't know what to do about it."

DeeDee set down a couple of platters of food. "You want anything to eat?" she asked me.

I shook my head. "No, I'm good, thanks."

"Where did Mr. Fancy-Pants go?"

"Off to be someone's happily-ever-after. Or at least, happily-for-tonight," I said.

"What?" DeeDee frowned. "Happily what?"

Stella laughed. "Never mind, DeeDee. Chris here is just jealous."

I stared into my beer. Was Mike ever going to issue an ass-back-ward invitation like that to me? Or *any* kind of invitation? "Damn straight I am." I muttered.

The next morning, Tyler slid the armoire into its place in the hallway, and it fit perfectly.

"Of course it fits," he said crossly, in response to my delighted applause. "Why wouldn't it?"

I carried the doors out to the front porch and sanded them by hand, getting into every crevice. I was wearing a bandana tied around my forehead to keep the sweat from dripping into the door. The porch would protect the doors from falling leaves or any other debris. Then I sanded the drawers, and after lunch, wiped them down with a tack cloth to remove all the sawdust, and then began to apply the stain. The fumes weren't terrible, and it took me a lot less time that I thought it would. When I was done, I looked across the street to see if Mike's truck was there so I could show off my handiwork.

His truck wasn't there. Neither was Steve's.

"Where's the boss?" I asked Tyler.

He shrugged. "There's somebody getting married this weekend, a cousin, I think. Steve insisted Mike get a new suit, and Mike insisted Steve come and help him." Tyler grinned. "They're like little kids, sometimes. It's pretty funny."

I'm sure it was, but that meant that I wouldn't be seeing Mike at all day today, and I had called the Medical Center and made an appointment to talk to someone about a job tomorrow, which meant I wouldn't see Mike until Friday...

That kind of took the glow out of my day. But the doors and the drawers of my armoire looked great.

After getting Tyler to swear he would bring them inside before he left for the day, I went back to Terri's, showered off, and walked out to the beach to sit under my umbrella and read until almost sunset, then went back, ate cold salad with Terri, and went to bed.

I drove up to the Northampton County Medical Center the next morning and filled out an application. I handed it to a rather harried-looking woman who glanced at it briefly, then frowned and read the whole thing again, much slower.

"You ran a real estate office?" she asked.

I nodded. "For twenty-five years."

"And you managed the whole thing by yourself?"

"No. I mean, yes, in the beginning. I had to do everything. But as the business grew, I hired people to do most of the clerical stuff."

"You have an appointment with Mr. Stall?"

"Yes. For ten-thirty. I'm a little early—"

"That's fine. I'll be right back." she said.

I nodded my head and sat.

What on earth was I doing here? I had no real interest in working in the medical field, which had always seemed to me to be shrouded in mysterious codes and abbreviations. On the other hand, I probably needed to work somewhere, because Terri hadn't found us a house to flip and I couldn't see myself sitting in my front porch waving at tourists for the next twenty years.

"Christiana?" I looked up. A tall man was hovering.

"Yes? Chris, Please."

"Chris? Fine. Can you come this way?"

I followed him through a maze of hallway to a cubicle half the size of my new front porch.

"I'm Darren Stall, and I'm the chief business administrator here, and one of our best people is leaving in September to have a baby and will not be coming back. You seem to have many of the skills required to do her job, which is very detail oriented and quite frankly, somewhat tedious. How are you with tedious?"

"Well. Let's see. Do you know anything about real estate? I completely memorized the regulations set forth by the Commonwealth of Virginia, so I've pretty much got tedious covered. I like details. I like everything to line up in a nice, neat little row."

He looked relieved. "That's the kind of person we need. This position is not really on the medical side as much as on the business side. It's only thirty hours a week, but we have a competitive salary and you'll be eligible for benefits after three months."

Did that mean health insurance? That was the one thing that had been as big a drain on my bank account as my house. "That sounds good," I said.

"You are going to stay here on the Eastern Shore, are you not?" he asked.

I nodded. "Yes. I have a house in Cape Edwards."

He looked relieved. "Good. You'd be surprised at the number of summer people who have come in and applied with no intention of staying through the winter. Something rather unexpected has come up today, and I apologize, but can you come for a more formal interview, say, early next week?"

"I'm going back to Rehoboth next week to finish up business," I told him. "The week after? Monday morning?"

We agreed on a time, shook hands, and I left the MedCenter is a daze. Had I really just gotten myself a job interview?

To celebrate, I drove north and shopped. After all, if I did have a job, I could splurge a bit, right? And I'd had my eye on these two lamps in a little shop in Exmore.

I texted Terri that I had a job interview, bought the lamps, a small side table, and a beautifully faded rug that would be perfect in the bedroom, dull green with cream and shades of rose. Then I found an antique quilt in the same colors, for way too much money. I debated with myself for about ten minutes, then went back to my mantra: Eat the cookie, take the chance, spend the money...

And I had job interview! That was almost a job. Who could I celebrate with?

The person I wanted to celebrate with was Mike, of course. I wanted us across the table from each other, laughing and drinking champagne, then walking out and down Main Street in the moonlight, my head on his shoulder...

I was halfway home when I pulled over on the shoulder of Rt. 31 and called Mike. And of course I got his voicemail. I leaned my forehead against the steering wheel, trying to decide between hanging up or leaving a silly 'just saying hi' kind of message, when it occurred to me that taking a bit of a chance on a voicemail was probably easier than in person.

"Mike? It's me. Chris. I applied for a job, and they want me to come back for an interview and I just felt like celebrating, and I was, you know, wondering if you'd like to buy me a drink tonight? Or I could buy you one. After all, I might be swimming in the big bucks pretty soon. So, well, anyway, I'll be down at Sam's on Main if you decide to join me."

I hung up and took a few deep breaths. That sounded just fine. Not desperate, because I really wasn't. After all, I didn't *need* him to congratulate myself on a good job prospect. And Sam's on Main was familiar territory—if he didn't show, I'd probably see at least one person I knew who might, in fact, want a drink.

I felt a whole lot better as I pulled back out, thinking I'd done a pretty good job, and then I realized I hadn't given him a time. So what did that mean? Should I call him back? No, I wasn't desperate. I had to remind myself of that.

I sat in traffic on Main Street, hoping I'd catch a glimpse of him at the job site, but I couldn't see his truck anywhere. So, I guess I'd be sitting in Sam's on Main until...when? When was an appropriate time to stop waiting for a date that really wasn't a date at all, just a casual invitation?

But I'd done it. I put myself out there, and even if he didn't show up at all, it was fine because I was just a little bit proud of myself.

A lone woman sitting on a bar stool on an evening in summer attracts way more attention than I would have reckoned. Especially since the woman was me, and I was not young, thin, or beautiful. Granted, my hair was behaving in the air-conditioning, and I had on lipstick and even mascara, but still.

After refusing two drinks in the first hour, I was ready to go back to Terri's and just pretend I'd never left Mike a voicemail in the first place. I started looking around for a familiar face, and wouldn't you know, the first one I saw was Daniel's

He came up and kissed my cheek. "Why are you sitting here alone? Are you taking another risk and trying to get picked up by a total stranger?"

I glared at him. "No. I'm waiting for Mike."

"Oh? He's meeting you? How lovely."

"I don't know. He might be."

Daniel waved at the bartender. "Do you have any Stoli? At all?"

The bartender nodded, and Daniel breathed a sigh of relief. "Stoli martini. *Very* dry. With a twist." He turned back to me. "What do you mean, he might be?"

"I invited him to join me for a drink, but it was on his voicemail, and I didn't specify a time, and...forget it. Daniel, you can now officially claim the title of my last boyfriend. I do not know how to do this anymore."

"Don't be ridiculous," he said. "You'll be fine. Mike is a gentleman. I think you're very well suited. I'm sure he'll be here."

He accepted his drink, took a sip, and sighed with pleasure. "At last. It's almost perfect."

"Marie drinks those," I said just making conversation.

"I know. I made her one or three last night." He shifted his drink to his other hand so he could lean his elbow against the bar. "She is a charming woman. Just charming. And quite bright, you know. I like smart women."

"Chloe?" I said, raising an eyebrow

He rolled his eyes. "You did know that she went to Brown, right? Granted, I don't think Chloe has much common sense, but...well, look, it's Mike!"

I turned to look toward the door, and yes, there he was. His eyes swept the room, found me, and lifted a hand.

And there I was, right next to my ex, and Mike had no way of knowing were actually talking about his current girlfriend, or possibly, his *future* girlfriend...

Daniel straightened and nodded to Mike as he came up and shook his hand. He knew me well enough to know exactly what I'd be worried about and came to the rescue. "Chris and I were just having a conversation about the current woman in my life. I suppose it's good to get a different perspective."

Mike shot me a look. "Chris a bit jealous?"

I almost spit out my drink.

Daniel just smiled. "Heavens no. More like celebrating her status as someone who no longer gives a damn."

"I heard a bit of something about you buying the Montecorvo place?" Mike said, grinning.

Daniel glared at me. "Yes, but please try to keep it under your hat."

Mike shook his head. "No worries. I heard directly from Celeste. She called me to tell me how happy she was, and what a wonderful person you were, Daniel."

Daniel could always lie gracefully. "Well, she's...lovely. And now, I really have to go. Night." He downed the rest of his drink in a gulp and left.

Mike looked down at me, and then looked around. "Where is everybody?"

He was wearing khaki shorts and a button-down shirt, sleeves rolled up, and I found myself staring at those forearms again, and his hands...

"What? Oh, there's no everybody. It's just us." I was a bit breathless when I said it, because I knew that his reaction would mean a great deal. I swallowed hard as he frowned slightly, then his eyes began to twinkle.

"Just us? Well, what do you know about that? " he said slowly, starting to smile. "It's funny, though, because Steve had said that you didn't want to be going out without your...what was the word he used? Entourage?"

I'd gotten this far. I'd left him the message that got him through the door, and he was right there, in front of me, and if I didn't take the step right now...

I looked straight at him. "I told him that because I didn't want to hurt his feelings by just saying that I didn't want to be going out *him*."

Mike raised his eyebrows. "Is that so?"

I swallowed hard. "Yes. Because I wanted to go out with you."

He grinned. "Is that so?"

My heart was pounding so loud and so fast I was sure that every single person in the bar could hear it, and I glanced around to see if anyone had begun to stare at me yet.

"Charlie," Mike called. "Put this here lady's drink on my tab, and do you have any champagne back there? Cold?"

The bartender gave Mike a funny look. "You can't be drinking from open bottles on the street, Mike. You know that."

"Yes, I do. But this fine woman and I are going to walk over to the marina and open that bottle on my boat. There's nothing wrong with that, is there?"

I looked up at Mike. "Your boat?"

Mike was chuckling and shaking his head. "Yep. She's not much, more of a fishing dinghy, if you must know, but she's a perfectly good place to drink champagne."

He took the bottle and slid his hand on my back as we wound our way to the front door and on to Main Street. He stopped at the curb, looked up and down the street and grabbed my hand.

"Run. Quick before some idiot runs us both down."

I didn't run, I flew, and he kept my hand all the way to the marina and down the dock until we reached a low, gently rocking shape in the water. He jumped in, set down the bottle, and held out both hands to me.

"Come on, I'll catch you."

I stepped, and he caught me all right, and he pulled me to him and his arms went around me, and our lips met and I swear, somewhere, I heard a choir start to sing.

"I was wondering," he finally said in a low voice, "if we were ever going to do this."

I tried to speak, but found I had to take a breath, so I nodded instead and kissed him a second time. His lips were just as soft as I'd imagined them to be, and the kiss deepened and all sorts of interesting thoughts started going through my head, like what did the *inside* of his boat look like?

I finally pulled away. "So," I said, my voice a little hoarse, "is this boat one of those cabin cruiser things?"

He tightened his arms around me and laughed. "No, I'm afraid not. At all. But I do have these two nice leather seats right here and a couple of red plastic cups stashed in the cooler. Why don't we drink a little and talk about this?"

I slid down and sat while he rummaged through something along the side, coming up with red cups. He sat beside me and popped the champagne cork There was a loud noise and a wisp of something in the semidarkness.

"Now, a little for you, and little for me?" He poured, set the bottle down, and kissed me again, very light and quick. "We have a few things to celebrate, don't we?"

The champagne was sweet and bubbly and cold and perfect, and I wanted him to lie down in the bottom of the boat so I could pour the rest of the bottle over him, and slowly lick the champagne off...

"So what should we drink to?" he asked.

"How about taking chances?" I said, smiling at him.

He bent close. "I will take a chance on you any day, Chris Polittano," and we clicked our glasses together, and drank, and kissed a bit more before his arm went around my shoulder and I settled against him, my head alongside his, looking up at the stars.

"I'm thinking," he said, "that maybe you and I should have a nice dinner somewhere. In fact, I happen to be a pretty good cook. You could drive over to my place, and I could grill us something amazing, then we can have a bit of wine, watch the water? How does that sound?"

"It sounds perfect." And it did—perfect and romantic and just the two of us. "You live on the water?"

"Technically speaking, on Mockhorn Bay. You take Seaside Road going south till you get to the dead oak tree—no, I'm not kidding—and turn toward the water. I have a little bit of river, then a bit of marsh, and then Mockhorn, and eventually, the Atlantic. Quite a view."

I laughed and pressed myself against his side. Had I ever felt this happy and safe? That was it. I felt safe. I also felt...empowered.

All my life, every man I'd been with had pursued me, and I'd felt flattered by the attention. I'd also felt obligated to follow them to the next step, and after I had, none of those other men ended up making me happy.

But Mike was someone I'd seen and wanted, just for myself, and I'd gone after him. Sure, it had taken me a while, and the whole time, in the back of my head I worried that he wouldn't return my feelings. But I'd taken the risk and here was the payoff: sitting with him on a summer's evening, his arm around me in the moonlight. And more than anything else, I knew him to be a good man, and I was willing to trust him with not just my home, but my heart.

"Sounds...perfect. How about tomorrow night?" I suggested.

He shook his head. "My cousin's son, Charles Eli McCann, is getting married on Saturday, and Steve and I are of course invited to the bachelor party and all the other parties involved. We leave tomorrow morning for Roanoke. But I'll be back Sunday evening."

"Sunday I have to drive to Rehoboth. Closing Mom's house, finishing some final stuff for my business. But I can be back Thursday. Afternoon."

He laughed and poured more champagne." Afternoon, eh? Why that sounds positively decadent. Then I guess we wait until next week."

I pouted into my red plastic cup. "A whole week?"

He kissed me, very slow and deliberate, and my toes curled. "I think we can wait a whole week. A little aging sweetens the wine?"

I bit his lower lip and tugged gently. "Sweeten away."

I could see his eyes dance in the moonlight and heard the happiness in his voice. "You know that I've kinda wanted you from the very first time I saw you."

"Kinda?"

"Well, I did want to wait and see if it was just lust or something more."

"And?"

"Pure lust. And a whole lot more."

"Yeah. Me too." I ran my fingers down the front of his chest, and it took everything I had to keep from unbuttoning his shirt so I could press my fingers against his skin. His lips were in my hair, and against my throat, and his hand slid up the inside of my knee as I turned and tried to climb on top of him...

The boat took a sudden dip, and the champagne bottle rolled from one side of the boat both to another.

"We spilled our champagne," he whispered.

"I don't care," I said, and kissed him again.

Chapter Nine

I 'm sure I did things on Friday. Terri kept looking at me strangely, and I know that I smiled a lot. Saturday was pretty much the same. And Sunday, I got in my car and drove all the way back to Rehoboth. I don't remember doing the actual driving though, just like I didn't really remember Friday or Saturday, because my brain was stuffed with Mike McCann, and the way his lips tasted, and the feel of his hands, and how soft his beard felt against my skin.

We texted back and forth, and every time my phone chimed, I jumped a foot. But it wasn't just because I was going to finally be with him, find out exactly what he could do with those strong and very capable hands and that delicious mouth. Whatever I was feeling for him, he had just the same intense feelings for me. And not just lust. More, *so* much more, and I was drowning in so many emotions I couldn't begin to sort them out. I just wanted to get back to him as fast as possible and have him grill me a bit of something, drink some wine, watch the water and enjoy whatever happened next.

Everything in Rehoboth went as planned. There were no last-minute legal glitches, and for my part, no seller's remorse. As I walked though the house for the last time, all the memories seemed faded and a bit sad. I was walking away from the whole of my past, and there would no longer be a home for me to run back to, as I'd done so many times before when things had not worked out for me. But I knew what my future looked like now, and I was happy and silly and impatient to be done with Rehoboth and everything it once meant.

Wednesday afternoon, as I was signing things that would officially end my involvement in Corner Street Realty, Terri sent me a text.

Dinner tonight with Steve! Invited him to talk about the house but—

There followed a series of heart emojis. As soon as I'd shaken hands with everyone for the last time, I called her.

"Terri. Listen to me very carefully. Tonight, when you're with Steve, keep it business only."

I could practically hear her roll her eyes. "Chris, the last thing I want to talk about is that house."

"I know. But listen to me. Remember how I told you that every woman who's ever made a play for him hasn't lasted?"

"And I said—"

"I know what you said. But he told me that the women around here expected him to act a certain way, and he didn't sound like he was all that thrilled about it."

"What are you talking about?"

"Tonight just talk about the house. No personal questions, no flirting, no trying to see deep into his soul. Be detached and impersonal."

"And where, exactly, do you think that will get me?"

"Hopefully the same place it got me. With him a little intrigued."

She was silent. "I'm not so good a playing hard to get."

"Don't play hard to get. Just don't throw yourself at him. And if he issues an invitation, decline."

"What? But...really?"

"Really. Tell him you'd rather get to know him better."

"And you think that will work?"

"Saying yes on the first ask hasn't worked for anyone else, Terri."

"Hmm...okay. Maybe you're right. All business."

I breathed a sigh of relief. I wanted Terri and Steve to get together, not because I thought it was such a good idea, but because she was my friend and it was what she wanted.

"One more thing," I said.

I heard her sigh. "What?"

"Be sure you look amazing," I told her.

She laughed. "Oh, honey, I always look amazing."

Then she hung up.

Thursday morning I got a text from Mike.

Make sure you find me as soon as you're home we have to talk

I thought it was odd but pushed it from my mind. I was on my way back. I'd be there around three, just in time to take a shower, shave my legs because *expectations*, and drive over to his place for a bit of something-something.

I practically flew down the highway, which, considering the tourist traffic, was a lot harder than it should have been.

I made it to Terri's just before four and flew up the stairs. As I was turning the key in the lock, I heard Daniel's voice above me.

"Chris? Is that you? What in the hell is going on?"

I dumped my overnight bag in Terri's front hall and went upstairs.

He was pacing in front of his open door. "I've been here all afternoon waiting for you to get back."

"Why didn't you text me?"

"I did. Several times. Do you still have that useless Do Not Disturb While Driving thing on your phone?"

I pulled my phone out of my shorts pocket and looked. Sure enough, six texts from Daniel, all saying the same thing: *RUHOMEYET???*

I took a breath. "Sorry. What's going on?"

"Ryan came down this morning to walk the Montecorvo property with me," Daniel began. Ryan was the banker that had worked with Daniel for almost ten years.

"He didn't want to give you the money?" I asked.

"No, don't be silly. Of course he was going to give me the money. He loved it. And then I walked him to the car, and waved goodbye, and Celeste came running out, in tears, saying that she was selling to Amy McCann after all, and she was sorry, but that was what Mike told her to do, and she trusted Mike and knew there had to be a good reason. So. I was out of the picture."

"Wait." I walked across to the couch and sat slowly. "She said that Mike told her to sell to *Amy?*"

He followed me and sat next to me, his jaw clenched. "Mike apparently made a deal."

I sat in silence. How could Mike possibly do something like that?

"I don't understand," I croaked. "Did you talk to Mike?"

Yes, and he was a real SOB about the whole thing, saying he had his reasons. End of story. So now, I have to call Ryan back—"

I shot out my hand. "Not yet. There has to be a mistake. Mike wouldn't make a deal with Amy. Don't tell Ryan anything yet. Let me talk to Mike and find out what's going on."

I felt all the joy rushing out of me. What had happened in the short time we'd been apart? Had he and Amy met and...talked? Had they, in fact, made some sort of deal?

Had they gotten back together?

"Chris? Listen, I'm sorry, please, don't be upset." Daniel reached for my hand and patted it briskly "God, you look awful. It's only a business deal, I shouldn't have made such a stink. Do you need a glass of water? I'll get you some water. Please, don't faint."

I gripped his hand. I felt how icy my skin was against his, and I really did feel sick. Physically ill. My stomach turned and I couldn't catch my breath.

Was Mike back with her? Is that what his odd text was about this morning? Here I thought I knew him. Obviously, I didn't know him at all. Was he really just going to be another bad mistake of mine?

I stood up. "I have to find Mike."

"Are you sure you're all right? Let me drive you—"

"No." I brushed him off. "I'm fine. I just need to talk to Mike."

I went back downstairs, locked Terri's front door, and went back out to the street.

I pulled in behind the retail site on Main Street. It was late, but there were still a few men around. No, Mike wasn't there, they told me. He'd gone home early.

I glanced across the street and could see Terri through the front window, talking to Steve. She was laughing, and he had his head bent down to hers. I'd been gone almost a week, and Terri had sent me pictures of all she'd gotten done at the house, but I didn't even care.

I typed Seaside Road into the GPS and headed across the island. Away from the bay, things got rural in Northampton County, and Seaside Road was not so much about the sea as it was about farmland and dust. Yes, there was a dead oak tree by a turnoff, so I took the turn and bumped my way along until I came to a sprawling ranch house under oaks hung with Spanish moss. I turned off the car and took a breath.

What was I going to say to him?

I got out of the car and heard a wild yapping. Joe came racing around from the back of the house and skid to a halt at my feet, tail wagging, a doggy-smile on his face. I bent to rub his ears, then went up the walk to the porch and knocked on the door.

"Mike?"

I waited, still not knowing how I was going to even start this conversation. Hey, Mike, are you sleeping with your ex-wife again? Is that why you turned Daniel's deal upside down? Because, really, what other reason could there be?

"Mike?" I called again and pushed open the screen door.

I could look right through his living room to a wall of sliding glass doors that overlooked the marsh, with a winding bit of silver going through it before disappearing into the woods. The glass doors were open, and the air was warm and smelled of salt. I took a few steps in. I could watch this all day, I thought. The sea grass waved in the breeze and a giant white bird appeared from nowhere, cutting across the evening sky.

"Chris?"

He'd obviously just come from the shower, his jeans low on his hips, his broad chest and shoulders still damp. Any other day I would have leapt across the room and tackled him to the floor. Now, all I wanted to do was yell.

"What did you do?" I said loudly, my voice shaking. I felt the world around me had cracked, somehow. If this man, who I had believed to be so good, could turn against Celeste and Connie to make a deal with Amy...

He crossed the room quickly, grabbed both of my arms, and tried to move me, but I broke away from him and hit him, hard, with both of my fists against his chest.

"What did you do?" I screamed. I fought to bring my voice under control. I was angry and hurt and felt completely betrayed. I had trusted him. "It was a done deal, Mike. Daniel was going to build, Celeste and Connie were going to get their money, and nothing was going to be bulldozed and covered in concrete. It was *done*."

He shook his head. "I know."

"You made a deal with *Amy?*"

"It's not how it sounds."

"Really? Good, cause it sounds like something changed your mind, and the only reason I could think of for your doing that was because you'd slept with her."

"No. God, no." He was trying to hold me again, but I kept pushing his hands away.

"How could you do this to those two sweet old women, Mike? They trusted you, and you're going to take everything that they wanted away from them. What possible reason could there be for that?"

"You," he said simply.

"Me? What on earth are you talking about?"

"Amy called me this morning. It seems she is planning on buying lot right next door to your house."

I took a step back and sank down into the couch.

"The lot next door? Dr. Wilson's house?"

He shook his head. "No. The vacant lot." He sat across from me on the coffee table and took both my hands in his. "She called me first thing. Said she found the owner up in Vermont somewhere and has made an offer, and he's accepted. She was going to send him some sort of contract today. By Monday, she'll probably have it back."

I rocked back, pulling my hands with me. "Why would she do that?"

"She said that if the deal didn't go through with Celeste, she'd build a four-story commercial building right next door to you."

I shook my head. "She wouldn't be able to do that, would she?"

He took a breath. "All of Main Street is zoned commercial, Chris. About twenty years ago, the hotel on Main Street burned to the ground, and since it was four stories tall, she can make the case for another four-story hotel."

"She said she wanted a *hotel?*"

He nodded again. "In fact, she said she figured she could get twelve, maybe fourteen units in."

"That's a lot of people."

"Yes, Chris, it is."

"And lot of noise."

"A *lot* of noise."

"If she built something that tall, my house would be in a shadow all morning."

He tightened his lips. "I know." He took my hands again. "Chris, I love those two old women, I really do. And I wanted them to have their little bit of a dream come true. But I talked to Celeste this morning and told her what was going on. It was her decision. She didn't want your new home to be sitting right next to something like that. So, the deal is, when Amy buys the Coop, she's selling the lot to Celeste. And Celeste said she'd give it to you."

I felt the tears start, bitter and angry. How dare she? *How dare she?* I wanted to cry. I wanted to yell. I wanted to find Amy McCann and scream in her face.

"Well, can't *we* find the owner and buy that lot? I could make him an offer, you know. I have money from my mom's house."

"I don't know how she found him. We tried, remember? And she's not going to give me his name and address, I can guarantee that. "

"No, *you* tried. I can find him. Just give me a few days."

"We don't have a few days," he said softly. "And besides Chris, Amy is a commercial developer. Which means her pockets go deep. And whatever you offered, she'd top, and in the end, I don't see you winning." He reached up and wiped the tears that were running down my cheeks. "Celeste understands. She's okay with it. She told me that your future here is more important than her past."

"But she and Connie wanted to live there," I said, my voice breaking.

He moved next to me on the couch and put both arms around me. "They'll find a great place to live, Chris, you know they will. It's okay."

"No, it's not," I cried, and my whole body shook, my breath coming in deep, gulping sobs. I was so angry that one woman could come in and so easily topple everything I had carefully planned. I was also relieved that Mike had not, in fact, betrayed my trust. In fact, he did what he had to for me...

He held me, his lips pressed against my hair until the crying finally stopped and I was still, sniffling in the circle of his arms.

His thumb grazed my cheek as he wiped the tears again, and then he kissed me, little, tender kisses that grew, and my arms went around him.

I still wanted to cry. I still wanted to yell.

But more than all that, I wanted Mike.

In the beginning, we were gentle with each other.

His bed was huge and faced the marsh, and the sunlight filtered through the trees, so we didn't need to turn on a light. There was just enough for me to scar that ran along the back of his thigh, and the small heart-shaped tattoo on his hip.

His beard was soft and his hands were gentle for all their strength. We talked to each other: How does this feel? Is this good? How about now?

At one point he raised himself of his elbows, his face suddenly still. "I'm afraid I'm going to crush you," he whispered. I just tightened my legs around him and drew him even closer. We began in a slow and tender dance but ended with the both of us breathless and drained, curled together, his arms around me and his mouth against the back of my neck.

"I knew it," he said at last. " 'Though she be but little, she is fierce.' "

I rolled over to face him, our noses almost touching. "I didn't think you'd be so..."

He cracked a smile. "So...what?" His grin broadened. "Godlike?"

"Tender."

He kissed the tip of my nose. "I was seriously afraid I'd break something somewhere."

I shook my head. "I'm pretty tough."

"I know." His hand trailed down my back. "I believe the original invitation was for dinner?"

I nodded. "Yes, it was. But I think we both knew what we really wanted." I smiled. "However..."

He grinned and gave me a loud, sloppy kiss. "I have two beautiful steaks. And I'm in sore need of nourishment, woman. You practically wore me out."

He rolled out of bed and I watched him as he pulled on his jeans.

"Can I shower? I came over here right from being on the road."

"Ah, that's why you were salty as well as sweet. Sure, right through there."

I showered and rummaged through one of his drawers until I found a faded t-shirt. I pulled it on and padded out, through the living room and out to the deck.

He glanced at me and grinned. "I knew there'd be a good use for that ratty old shirt. You're gorgeous when you're all dripping like that."

"Well, it's a look. Can I help?"

He shook his head. "Nope. Just sit and have some wine and tell me the story of your life."

So I sat and I told him, and we ate juicy steaks with fresh sliced tomatoes and drank some more wine.

"That was delicious," I said when I finally pushed my plate away. "How did you manage to stay single for so long again?"

He laughed and poured me a bit more wine. "I was gun-shy after Amy. Didn't even date. I'm not whatchacall a social animal anyway. Never did the Friday night thing on Main Street. Just as soon take the boat out into the bay and fish. Or come home and look at the marsh and watch the birds. In the fall, lots of migratory birds come through here. Some days the sky is practically black with them. You'll have to come out and see them."

"I will," I said. I had pretty much decided that I was willing to just about anything he suggested. After what we'd just gone through, I knew that all his ideas were pretty spot on.

"So, I hate to bring up a prickly subject," I began.

He threw his head back and laughed. "We've just made love six ways to Sunday. What on earth can you possibly be embarrassed about?"

"Steve," I said, taking a quick sip of wine.

He settled back in his chair. "Funny thing about Steve. He had dinner with your friend Terri last night, and that's kind of all he talked about today."

"Really?" I said. I gave Terri a mental high five for obviously sticking to the plan.

"Really. I wasn't paying too much attention, understand. I did have a thing or two on my mind, but it seemed to me he thought she was not at all what he expected." It was dark now, and the only light was from the solar lights around the deck, but I could see his face in the shadows. "I don't even think he knows what he wants from a woman. Or from life in general. He sees things he likes, and point and smiles and says, *yes, please*, but he's never really happy once he's got it." He shook his head. "I told him about us. Right away. He said he knew I was interested, he just couldn't understand why he was the one getting the short end of the stick. My brother is a terrific guy, but his ego tends to get a bit out of hand."

"Well, that's good. I didn't want there to by any broken bro-code thing to get in the way."

He was looking at me through half-shut eyes, smiling. "After that first kiss, nothing in this world could have gotten in my way. I just can't believe we wasted so much time dancing around each other."

"It was a good dance," I said. "It gave me a chance to know you better. And to decide if you were really what I wanted." I flashed a smile. "You are, by the way."

"Why, thank you, ma'am."

"Tomorrow call Amy and tell her that I've decided that she can buy the lot. I don't care what she builds there. I may have a way to stop her. Or I can fight her during a zoning board meeting. If I lose, I lose. But I'll be damned if I'm going to let have her way."

He froze, the wine glass halfway to his lips. "Seriously?"

"Yes."

"You're taking an awful chance there, Chris. She's a vindictive woman. She might very well go out of her way to put up the biggest, ugliest building Cape Edwards has ever seen."

"Maybe."

He leaned forward. "We're talking about your house."

I shook my head. "We're talking about my home, Mike, and a home is more than a building, and where it is and what it looks like. And my *home* is here, with Terri and Judd and Stella, with maybe a new job, and you." I smiled. "And Joe." At the sound of his name, Joe lifted his head and wagged his tail. "She can't ruin that for me. No one can. And anyway, all my risks have paid off so far. My derelict house is beautiful, my *aw, shucks* contractor is a tiger..." I stretched out my legs and wiggled my toes. Every inch of my body felt stroked and satisfied. "I hope you don't mind my saying, but for an old guy you're pretty hot."

"Old guy? *Old guy?* Chris, you cut me to the quick."

I grinned at him. "Yes, well, I've heard that some men, as they get a little older, tend to slow down a bit."

"Welp, I'm in construction. Spend a lot of time with those young bucks. All that testosterone rubs off, you know?" He held up his arm and showed me his muscle, Popeye style. His eyes twinkled. "You're pretty hot yourself, you know. For practically senior citizens, we're a pretty good team."

I felt my cheeks get hot. "Well, on my part, it was weeks of pent-up frustration."

He cocked his head to one side. "Really?"

"Yes sir. All that strutting around you did at the job site..."

"Strutting? That was my natural swagger."

I laughed. "Whatever. It certainly worked."

He sighed and stretched out his arms. "Yep. I still got it."

I reached over with my foot and kicked him, and he caught my eye and laughed.

The rest of the evening was like that. Patter. Jokes. Laughter and a little more wine. He didn't suggest I go home, and in the morning, the sunrise through his bedroom window woke me, and I walked out to the deck to the sound of birds calling as the marsh came alive, and then he came up behind me, and wrapped his arms around me, and we watched as the new day began.

Terri was laying pavers in my back patio when I finally arrived that morning. She was carefully leveling the sand, and gently placing the paver in place, tapping it with a rubber mallet. I watched her for a few minutes.

"You're good at that," I said, a little surprised.

She jumped, glared at me, and stood up.

"And where were you last night?"

"With Mike. We had a few things to work out."

"I bet. Daniel came down last night in an absolute twist. You'd better talk to him right away before he says something vile to Mike."

I hadn't thought about that.

Mike had dropped me at Terri's so I could change, and I'd walked up. I hadn't seen Daniel at the site across the street, but then, I hadn't been looking for him. I hurried around to the front of the house, scampered across the street, and rounded the corner just in time to see Daniel nose-to-nose with Mike, as the crew all stood, watching the morning's entertainment.

"Daniel, a word?" I called.

He turned to me, glared back at Mike, and stalked—there was no other way to describe it—across the lot to where I stood.

"I was just giving him a piece of my mind," Daniel muttered. "What he's doing to those two wonderful women is bad enough, but if he thinks he can treat you—"

"Daniel, we're fine."

"Obviously, you care for him. And stupid me, I thought he actually cared for you as well. But then," he waved his hand. "What do I know?"

"Daniel, Mike and I are fine."

"And Marie filled me in on some of the things Amy McCann has done in the past, including being just a little sketchy with EPA—"

"Daniel. Stop."

He took a breath. "All right. I'll stop."

"Good. Now, go ahead with your funding. A deal is a deal."

He opened his mouth to say something, closed it, frowned, and tried again. "What?"

"You're buying from Celeste and Connie, just as planned." I told him briefly what Amy had told Mike and watched as his expression went from confusion to anger. "She'd do that?" he asked. "To punish you?"

I blew out some air. "Apparently. But I might be able to stop her. So I have a favor to ask."

He shrugged. "Ask away."

"Remember that conservation group that gave you such a hard time a few years back? Over..."

"Yes. Over a red-beaked something. They stopped construction, dragged me into court...what about them?"

"Well, let's say someone bought that empty lot, and wanted to build a four-story hotel on it. If a Delmarva fox squirrel had built a nest on one of those big old trees, and that squirrel was on the endangered list..."

"Then that same crackpot environmental group could very easily stampede into town and stop construction."

I grinned. "Exactly."

"Who owns that lot?"

"Doesn't matter. But Amy is planning on buying it."

He rolled his eyes. "Ever since I got here, I've found myself directly in her crosshairs. And it's been mostly your doing. Why are you doing this to me?"

"Because I know that you're not afraid of a fight."

"But must you *push* me into the ring?"

"Daniel, I got you Celeste. I'm going to make sure that you get your medical park, Celeste gets her assisted living, and hopefully, I'll get nice little house with a big empty lot next door. Please?"

He sighed and rolled his eyes. "Yes, of course. Delmarva fox squirrel? Good Lord. Okay, I'll let you know when I find out anything." He straightened, rolled his shoulders and walked back to Mike. A few words were exchanged, and Mike clapped him on the back. The crew looked disappointed, and they all began to get back to work.

Mike came up to me, his eyes dancing. "So, Daniel won't challenge me to pistols at fifty paces tomorrow morning?"

I grabbed his shirt and pulled him close, standing on my toes to reach his mouth. "I just saved you, big time. Isn't my kitchen coming today?"

"Yes, I believe around noon. And then next week the marathon starts. The floor goes in, the rest of the lighting, painting, and the countertop is supposed to be in by Friday. I'll try to get over there and help as much as I can. You need to all your appliances delivered. We have your final inspection week after next."

"When can I deliver my bed?"

"I'd wait at least until the floor goes in. Why? Do you feel a pressing need for a new bed?"

"Maybe. See you later."

I was floating. I was flying. I was happy and I can't remember a time that I'd felt so hopeful about the future.

But I knew that my happiness all depended on the super-squirrel, Bella.

I watched them install my kitchen cabinets, then I finished putting in all the shelving I'd ordered for my new hall closet armoire. I had a few screws left over, but Steve looked at it, said everything seemed good and sturdy, so I tossed the leftovers in the dumpster.

Later in the afternoon, Mike brought Joe over, and he and I and Terri and Steve sat on the porch and talked paint color. I must have had twenty or thirty samples, representing everything from the outside trim to the inside of the guest room closet.

Mike and Steve exchanged a look, and Steve cleared his throat. "We only have painters scheduled one day for the inside, and one day for the outside. You might want to pare down your choices."

"But Chris and I can also paint," Terri said.

Steve grinned at her. "Yes, you can, and I'm sure the two of you would do a great job. But don't you have to go back to work? Or do you have another week or two of vacation left?"

She made a face. "No, I don't. I spent two weeks in Antigua back in February."

I'd been watching her with Steve and was impressed with how she acted around him. Considering how eager she'd been to be finally spending time with him, she was rather reserved with him, friendly but not fawning, interested in what he had to say without drooling all over him. And it seemed to be having an effect. He was attentive to her, much more than he'd been earlier in the summer.

"You've got all sorts of corners and angles," Mike pointed out. "You might want to just go basic." He spread out the samples, finally drawing one out. "How about the whole thing just a simple cream."

I looked at Vanilla Bean #4, got up and stood in the front doorway and looked into my house. I imagined all the drywall painted over, the few hanging wires tucked away, and saw everything as a clean, calm whole. My couch was blue-gray, and the floors were going to be a pale maple. I'd found the perfect rug: cream with shades of blue and touches of beige and faded red, the same red as the legs of my kitchen worktable. Everything clicked: my house would be the colors of the sand and the shells, with the gray of the sky and the cool blue of the bay.

"Deal," I said.

"Good," Mike said. "I'll even help. Steve, you can look after what's going on across the street next week? Let me spend a little time over here?"

Steve nodded. "Sure."

Joe trotted down off the porch, lifted his leg against my one azalea bush, and once again crossed into the vacant lot to sit in front of his favorite tree.

"There's something up there he wants," Mike said.

"Hopefully, it's the right kind of Bella," I said.

Steve frowned. "A what?"

I shook my head. "It's my one shot of not having a NoTell Motel next door."

Later, I left Terri to her Friday night regulars, and Mike and I went out on his boat. We sat, just talking, until the sun went down.

"I can see why you'd rather spend your evenings out here," I told him. "It's beautiful. And peaceful."

"Yep," he said. "I do my best thinking out here."

"I'm going out to see Celeste tomorrow and tell her the deal is back on with Daniel."

He exhaled loudly. "You're sure?"

I nodded.

"You gonna tell me what it is you think you can pull off?"

"Nope. It's a long shot, and I'd just as soon wait it out alone."

We pulled into the marina late, and he helped me from the boat, and we walked, hand-in-hand toward Main Street.

"Want to stop somewhere for a drink? Say hello to some people?" he asked.

I shook my head. "No, thanks. I'm good. '

"Want to go back to my place? See if we can recreate a little night magic?"

I grinned. "That sounds perfect."

But we ended up falling asleep on his couch, arms around each other, and when he woke me, it was after midnight, so we went to bed and just held each other until we were both asleep again.

That was also perfect.

Chapter Ten

C eleste did not seem very confident of my plan.
"It's a squirrel," she said. "They're like rats with fluffy tails."

"It's a Delmarva fox squirrel and she's on the endangered list. Which means Amy won't be able to cut down any of the trees."

Celeste squinted at me. "You sure that's what it really is? And not some mutant regular rat with a fluffy tail?"

"My neighbor, Miss Ava, told me, and I think she knows exactly what she's talking about."

Celeste looked impressed. "Miss Ava at the Nature Center? She knows a lot about the animals around here." She peered at me through her thick lashes. "Let's take a walk," she said.

I'd walked her property enough times before that I knew her favorite places: a rose bush she'd planted years ago at the base of a towering pine that had grown so far up the trunk looking for sunlight that when it bloomed, the entire top of the tree was covered in blazing red flowers. There was a small open space in the trees where daisies bloomed. And she'd planted azaleas around a massive boulder, and they had grown so large that, last time I'd been there, it looked as though the rock was crawling out of the brilliant pink flowers.

"Daniel, he won't cut this down?"

I shook my head. "Celeste, you made him draw out his plans, remember? He wants to save as much as he can. And he will. He believes that parking lots should have shade, and that balconies should look out on something other than blacktop."

She stopped and picked a small wildflower, holding it to her nose. "Mike almost broke my heart when he called me."

"I'm sure."

"That Amy woman is a bitch. We need to get her."

"We're going to, Celeste. Want to drive out to talk to Connie?"

"Not today. I worked all day, and I'm done. I'll see her tomorrow and let her know what's happening." She lay her hand on my arm. "What if—"

I bent to kiss her cheek. "So far, my luck has been running with me. Celeste. I'm willing to take one more chance."

She patted my cheek. "Okay then. I'll send you all my good juju."

"You do that, Celeste. You do that."

The final week at the house was a whirlwind.

First thing Monday morning I went back to the MedCenter. The interview, I thought, went well. I'd spent two hours in front of the administrative board, and they'd given me a very detailed picture of what the job was and how they expected it to be done. Darren had been right, there'd be lots of tedious paperwork. That hadn't been my favorite part of the real estate business, but I'd been good at it. For a modest salary and health insurance, I would be grateful for the job.

Darren shook my hand warmly after the interview and leaned in to whisper in my ear. "The other three candidates were impossible. You're our last interview, and I think you've got this. I'll call you when we reach a decision."

When I got to the house, the floor went in, pale golden planks that I held in place as Tyler nailed them to the subfloor. Then, the baseboard and moldings went up, like frames around a canvas. On Wednesday, while the outside was being spray painted a soft sage green, Mike and I painted the bedrooms, while hired painters stood on scaffolding with sprayers to paint the tall ceilings on the living areas.

"My bed is coming today," I told Mike. We were on the porch, eating lunch. Joe was at my side, watching every move as I ate my sandwich.

"Really? King size, I hope."

I raised an eyebrow. "No. Mike, you *built* that room. You know how much space there is. We'll have to make due with queen."

He swore softly and shook his head. "I'll have to modify some of my best moves."

I almost choked on my sandwich, laughing. He pounded me on the back as Joe stole the pickle right out of my bag.

"You do know that, technically speaking, you can't spend the whole night here until that final inspection," Mike said when he'd stopped laughing.

"Well then, we'd better speed up some of those moves of yours, okay?"

He kissed me. "I'm sure we can adapt."

Daniel came over when he saw us. He still wore a suit to the job site every day and looked as cool and polished as sea glass.

"Well, my source tells me that if indeed a Delmarva fox squirrel has made a nest in those trees, he and his group are fully prepared to build a human wall around the whole lot to prevent a single limb from being cut."

Mike looked at Daniel, then me, his expression one of complete confusion. "What are you even talking about?"

On cue, I saw Miss Ava coming down the sidewalk, a straw hat her head, her simple dress blowing behind her in the breeze. I jumped off the porch.

"Miss Ava, do you have a minute?"

She shook her head. "Late for a meeting, sorry." She waved as she climbed her front steps.

I ran down the sidewalk. "But it's about Bella."

She stopped dead and turned to look at me, her eyes narrow. "What about her?"

"She's a Delmarva fox squirrel?"

Miss Ava nodded.

"Are you sure?"

She drew herself up and put her hands on her hips. "Of course I'm sure, child. It's my job to be sure."

I held up both of my hands. "Sorry. I just—well, I needed to be absolutely positive, because someone is trying to buy the lot and put up a—"

"What? Put up a *what?*" She scurried over to me. "Someone is going to build there? Well, they can't. She's still considered a threatened species by the Commonwealth. I'm certainly not going to let anyone—"

"Miss Ava," I said gently, laying my hand on her shoulder. "I know. We were just talking about it. As long as we're sure, we can stop her."

She sniffed. "I happen to be something of an expert, you know."

I grinned. "Yes, I do know. And thank you for that."

She looked at her watch and muttered to herself. "I have to get over to church, but I will draw up and affidavit right away and get hold of somebody over at Fish and Wildlife. We can't technically stop the sale, but we can certainly get an injunction against any future construction."

I wanted to kiss her, but just nodded. "Yes, ma'am."

She sniffed again, nodded curtly to Mike and Daniel, and went back up her own walkway into her house.

Mike watched me walk back to him. "Well?"

"Well, we have an endangered species living next door. Whatever you do, keep an eye on Joe. If Joe eats that squirrel, we're toast."

He threw back his head and laughed. "Oh, this is rich. This is just about perfect. Well now, I feel a whole lot better about this entire operation."

Daniel looked smug. "And did I hear you say something about not stopping the sale?"

I shrugged. "Buyer beware. If she was so hot to build around here, she should have covered all her bases. I'll be sure to let her know as soon as I find out the ink is dry."

"Marie is the one to talk to about this," Daniel said. "She seems to know everything that's happening. And going to happen.

"You're right about that," Mike said. "Marie's kind of a big deal around here in real estate."

"And she makes an incredible martini," Daniel added. He straightened his already perfect tie, a sure indication he was about to make a pitch. "So, I don't suppose that when this all goes through as planned, the McCann brothers would be interested in coming on board? I realize it's a much bigger job than you're used to, and you'll probably have to forgo any other work to focus on this, but...well, the offer is there if you want it."

Mike pursed his lips and nodded. "I'll talk to Steve. I'm sure we can make it work."

"Good. Good, well, okay then, enjoy the rest of your lunch. Christiana, I'm so glad this squirrel thing worked out for you."

"Me too."

"Yes. All right then." He turned and sprinted back across the street.

I nudged Mike with my foot. "Going big time, there, aren't you?"

He let out a low whistle. "I guess. We do have three or four renovations already scheduled for over the winter, but after that..." He stood up and wiped the crumbs from his hands. "Where's my brother?" he mumbled and went back in the house.

A delivery truck pulled up in front of the house, and I watched as my bed was pulled out of the back. I walked the delivery team through to the master bedroom and looked out the window. Mike and Steve were on my new back patio, deep in conversation. All of my linens and the antique bedspread were stashed in a bin in the walk-in closet, so I found the sheets and pillows, made up the bed, and was smoothing out the pillows when Mike called for me.

"In here," I yelled back.

He stood in the doorway. "Good thing we painted this room first," he said.

"Hey, I'm no fool. Everything good with Steve?"

He nodded. "We need to really talk this through with Daniel, of course. Getting the manpower is no problem. If we need to, we can bring men over from across the bay. Big times ahead for these two hammer-and-nail guys." He pulled me into his arms and kissed the top on my head. "And it looks like you're going to put Amy into a very tight corner."

"One that she won't be able to get out of," I promised.

He lifted my chin and kissed my mouth. As usual, I felt a surge of pure desire go though me. Too bad the crew was right outside that door...

"I'm proud of you, Chris. I don't know who you were before, but since you've been here I've seen a strong woman taking control of her life and doing whatever she can to help the people she cares about. It warms my heart to think that someday you might do as much for me."

"I *am* doing this for you. I'm not going to let Amy McCann ruin this for me. For us. This is my home now." I tugged on his shirt. "You're part of that, you know."

He nodded and his arms tightened around me. "You're a good woman, Chris. I'm thankful that you've let me in to your life.." He pulled back and his eyes twinkled. "Maybe we should let the crew go home a little early today? Try out that brand new bed of yours?"

I twisted away from him. "Not until that backsplash is finished."

He threw his head back and laughed. "Deal."

Terri was in agony. "Do you have any idea," she moaned, "what it's like to be sitting there, across from a man, pretending that all you really care about is some dumb house, and all you really want to *do* is tear his clothes off?"

It was Friday night, and we were at the Grove as usual. I looked over at her and rolled my eyes.

Karen smirked. "Chris doesn't seem to have that problem anymore," she said.

"No, I don't. But Terri, hon, I do empathize." I sipped my wine. Mike was at the monthly Chamber of Commerce dinner, where, he assured me, he would make sure to stay out of Amy's way.

"But it's paying off, I think," she went on. "When I mentioned looking at another house, he complimented me on all I'd learned while I was there last week. And he meant it!"

I gave her a look. "Another house?"

She nodded, her eyes bright. "I found it on Zillow, it's only about twenty minutes from here, and it looks *perfect*."

"Here we go," Karen muttered.

"Here we go where?" Stella asked, coming up with Dara French beside her.

"I found another house for Chris," Terri said.

"But Chris has a house," Stella said.

Terri waved her hand. "I know. I meant for Chris and *I*. To flip. We did such a good job with this one..."

"Terri, the McCann brothers did a good job," I pointed out.

She nodded. "And I'm sure they'll do just as good a job this next time. And with you and me being able to do more of the work, this place—"

"Terri, where is the money going to come from? After I pay off this construction loan, I want to bank a little money for security, not risk it on another project. And I have a job now," I reminded her. I'd gotten a call from Darren Stall that morning, formally offering me the position as assistant to the business manager, beginning two weeks from Monday. "And you did all your work on vacation. So, unless you're planning on taking an early retirement..."

She made a face.

Dara reached over with her wine glass to click it with mine. "And congratulations, by the way. Darren is very excited for you to start. I'm sure you'll be wonderful."

I smiled. "I'm going to try for efficient.

She beamed. "That will work too."

"I'm issuing the invitation now, even though I could still flunk my final inspection," I said loudly. "Open house at the new Casa Polittano a week from next Sunday. Everyone is invited."

Karen waggled her finger at me. "You just may have invited the whole town, you know."

I shrugged. "So what. If people want to come, they can come. I'm having Bogey's make some sandwiches, I'll get a keg of something— what do you think?"

Terri rolled her eyes. "I think you have to pass your inspection first, before you invite half the town."

Dara leaned in. "Two weeks ago I had *my* final inspection," she said in a low voice. "I baked cookies. I didn't offer them to anyone, of course. After all, one wouldn't want to have an innocent gesture perceived as a bribe of any sort. But the gentleman who inspected my house seemed very appreciative when he found them on the kitchen counter."

Terri made a face. "She's been baking at my place for the crew for weeks now. When I was there for my vacation, every morning they all looked at me like I was this terrible person for not feeding them."

I smiled at Dara. "Thanks for the tip. Chocolate chip, I think."

She raised her wine glass. "A universal favorite."

Maria and Daniel arrived together, and it struck me how alike they seemed—sleek, classy, slightly more urbane than the rest of us. Daniel was wearing loose fitting linen trousers and a tight T-shirt, with a narrow belt around his waist. Maria was in a simple sleeveless shirt-dress, the collar pulled up high, and very chichi sandals.

"They match," Terri whispered to me. I nodded. They certainly did.

Daniel caught my eye and smiled, as did Marie, and they made their way toward us.

"I must say, this weekly ritual has all the makings of some sort of cult thing," Daniel said. "Do you really do this *every* Friday?"

"I'm trying to go native," I told him.

"That's what I'm trying to avoid," he muttered.

Marie swore, very briefly and very softly, and I followed her gaze to the front door.

Amy McCann.

Her entrance to the Grove did not have the same effect on the crowd that it had on Mike and his crew. In fact, people barely blinked, except the usual looks that happen when a stunningly beautiful woman enters a room. Terri came behind me to whisper,

"Is that her?"

I nodded and sipped some wine. It tasted bitter in my mouth.

Daniel looked at me, then Marie. "What?"

I waved and smiled broadly. "Amy, come on over. I want you to meet some folks."

She was in a pantsuit, and I realized she had probably been at the same Chamber of Commerce dinner as Mike and Steve. She strode across the crowded room, a rather tense and angry look on her face.

I kept the smile pasted on my face. "Amy, I'd like you to meet Daniel Russo," I said as she opened her mouth to speak. "Daniel is the gentleman who beat you out of that retail property here in town. And I believe he's also getting the Montecorvo place?"

Daniel gave me the look of death before turning and giving her his most charming smile. "Delighted to meet you at last," he said, practically purring. "It's nice to see your competition in the flesh." His hand was out, so she shook it briefly before turning to me.

"I heard from Mike," she began...

"And you know Marie Wu, don't you?" I continued. "I imagine you've crossed paths with her at some point."

She narrowed her striking blue eyes. "Yes. Hello Marie. Listen, Mike—"

"And this is Terri Coburn. She's the one who talked me into moving down here in the first place. Terri, this is Mike's ex-wife."

Terri practically batted her eyelashes. "A pleasure," she said.

Amy looked down and took a deep breath. "Perhaps you and I could speak privately?" she said.

I shook my head. "No, I don't think so." I was back in my realtor mode, wrestling with a client who couldn't understand why the entire world had not bent to her will. "I'm really just trying to enjoy the Grove."

"I *will* buy that lot," she hissed.

I nodded. "Yes. And I understand you want a hotel? Well, I can certainly see the benefits to the town. After all, more tax revenue, more tourist dollars...why, all those pluses are hard to beat. Of course, all those people who could have been renting out their homes or condos will be a little upset, and I'm sure no one will appreciate the extra traffic and noise, and then there's the whole parking angle...where, exactly, are all those cars going to go? Or are you going to try to change the ordinance about overnight parking on the street?"

Daniel stuck his hands in his pockets and was watching, his eyes bright. He nudged Marie and whispered something in her, sending Marie into a fit of silent giggles.

"You don't care that's it's going to be right next door to your house?" She asked in a low, incredulous voice.

I shook my head. "You know what, Amy, I'm trying to be a team player. I'm part of Cape Edwards now, and what's good for the town is good for me."

Her jaw dropped, and I looked over her shoulder to see Mike come through the door, his face grim.

I handed her my half-empty wine glass. "There's Mike. Please, excuse me," I said as I walked off.

I gotta say, the man certainly knew how to wear a suit. Naked he was pretty appealing, but in a dark navy suit that brought out the blue in his eyes...

I stopped in front of him and whistled slowly. "Hey, big guy, you sure do clean up good."

He kept glaring at Amy. "What did she say?"

I shook my head and took him by the arm. "Nothing important. I take it your dinner is over? As much as I like the look of you all decked out, I bet you'd love to take that suit off and slip into something a bit more...accommodating." I stood on my toes to whisper in his ear. "Like me?"

He looked down and his mouth dropped open. "Damn, woman, I though I was going to have to run in here and rescue you."

I shook my head. "No, Mike. As much as I appreciate the gesture, I don't need rescuing. Now, what I do need, well, that's something we can talk about on the way over to your place."

He kissed me. "Woman, you are an absolute delight. Let's go and take care of that. Immediately."

I spent the weekend doing little things: attaching the knobs to my kitchen cabinets, touching up the paint, screwing the covers over the electrical sockets. I was a little nervous over that one, convinced that I'd slip and send the screwdriver straight into the wires, electrocuting myself. Mike listened to my concerns with a relatively straight face, then went ahead and did them all himself.

Terri and Steve opted to work outside, mostly raking stray debris. Roofing nails, apparently, secretly multiplied by night, as I had been raking them up myself for weeks. I could hear the two to them talking, no distinct words, but the low rumble of their voices and an occasional laugh. Mike and I worked together, not really talking much at all, but I was aware of him, his body, how he moved through the house, the energy in everything he did. Joe's nails clicked against the hardwood floor as he looked for a place to settle. He finally lay down in a patch of sunlight, streaming through the dining room windows, the windows that had not been there eight weeks before, the windows I had desperately tried to imagine.

It had all come together.

Late Sunday afternoon I was still looking for things to do, but Mike shook his head. "We're all done here, Chris. There is nothing left. And, if I say so, it's all perfect. You'll pass your inspection. No problem."

I still baked chocolate chip cookies at Terri's though, and Tuesday morning Mike and I walked through the house with a silent, grim-faced man who stopped six times at the kitchen counter to eat a cookie or two. We'd already passed all the preliminary inspections: every mechanical had a separate inspection, and I knew we were not only up to code, we were over and above. Still, the inspector looked in places I'd almost forgotten about: behind the water heater, down in the crawl space, under the new porch. He finally shook my hand and welcomed me to the neighborhood, saying I'd receive the paperwork in the mail in seven to ten days, but I could move in any time.

The bed was already there, of course, and had even been tried and found to be quite big enough. I called for the couch to be delivered, then all the other things I'd ordered online. Then I began the tedious process of taking everything out of my storage container, including my mother's rocking chair, and a small stepstool my father had built for himself, back in his high school shop class. Then there was everything I'd stashed in Terri's guest room closet: new dishes and flatware and all new kitchen appliances, although I had kept Mom's Kitchen Aid mixer, over thirty years old but still a workhorse.

Mike was busy across the street, as was Steve, but Karen and Judd helped one afternoon, and Stella and Dara spent an evening with me carrying boxes of books from the trunk of my car to the newly assembled bookshelves. It only took a few days for me to make it look exactly as I'd pictured it.

Daniel and Mike came over together, walking through. Daniel shook his head. "You lived with me for how long? And I never would have imagined that this is how you'd want your own home to look."

I shrugged. "I was happy with your things, Daniel. And now, I'm happy with my own."

Mike hugged me tightly. "This place is beautiful. I never knew the old you, but this is just what I'd expect from the woman I've come to know."

Daniel, bouncing on the end of the couch, made a face. "But I would have expected a wall of bright orange, or maybe a purple sink in the bathroom. Isn't this your year for taking risks?"

I laughed. "I've taken my share, Daniel. I'm quite happy to let things ride nice and easy for a bit."

He leaned back. "Speaking of which, I close in two weeks. Celeste wanted me to invite you."

"Sorry, I'm a working girl again. But I'll see her and Connie on Sunday. I've invited them to my housewarming."

Mike chuckled. "You've invited everyone to your housewarming. My crew is expecting to be fed, you know. You spoiled them rotten while they were here."

"Not to worry," I said. "Bogey's is doing all the cooking. And I'll put you in charge of the keg. That should take care of them, right?"

He grinned. "Yep."

We heard Joe barking. "He's after Bella again." I said. "He's a stubborn thing, isn't he?"

Mike kissed me. "Not so much stubborn as hopeful."

"Well, I hope he never catches her. As soon as he does, Amy could swing into action."

"As soon as Amy realizes that she's sitting with a piece of land she can't do a thing with, she'll try to sell it off fast. Course, she'd rather be buried on it than sell to you, but I think if an anonymous donation is made to the town, why, Cape Edwards will buy it up, just to keep old Bella safe from harm."

Daniel cleared his throat. "Anonymous donor?"

Mike nodded. "Celeste. She's already said she's good for it."

"Miss Ava will be pleased," I said.

Daniel looked exasperated. "All these small-town machinations are simply astounding."

"Well, you'd better get used to it," I said. "You'll be spending a lot of time here in the next year or two."

He looked suddenly smug and very self-satisfied. "Yes. As I matter of fact, I will."

Karen had been right. Apparently, I did invite the entire town, because people started showing up at the house just after noon, some of them total strangers, all of them eager to see what I'd done with the place. I shook my head in wonder as they wandered around my house, as though visiting a museum, some quite critical of my decorating choices. But quite a few people made comments about my armoire closet, telling me what a clever girl I'd been to think of that, so I really didn't mind all that much.

Judd arrived early to take his last round of pictures, and set up a slide show on his laptop, right on the kitchen island, with all the pictures he'd taken of the work-in-progress. I still couldn't believe the house had gone from a wreck of a shell to picture perfect in just two months.

I also couldn't believe I'd met and fallen in love with Mike McCann in that same amount of time.

Because I did love him, deeply and fiercely, a kind of feeling I hadn't had with any of the other men I'd loved before. Maybe it was because I was older now and realized how rare and precious it was to find someone at this stage of my life. Maybe it was because he had been the hardest won, someone I'd thought about and wondered about and yearned for, rather than have had him just drop at my feet. Or maybe because he was a rare man, a good man, and I knew how lucky I was to have him in my life. I hadn't said the words. I didn't dare. What I told Daniel about not taking any more risks was true. I wouldn't do anything that might upset our chances for a future, and until I knew he felt the same way, I would be happy just knowing that I was the one he wanted to be with.

Celeste and Connie arrived, and Mike pushed Connie's wheelchair around to the back patio, now furnished with weatherproof wicker and teak tables and chairs. I'd splurged at the last minute and in my haste to have everything perfect for the party, bought out all the floor samples at Lowes.

Celeste walked through the house, and she somehow found all the pieces I'd brought from Rehoboth: the older books and framed pictures, mom's embroidered pillow, and a picture my father had taken of a sailboat, simply sitting in the water, the sun behind it. It was almost a perfect composition, and he'd framed it, and now it hung in my hallway.

"You can tell the new things from the old," Celeste said. "New things shout, hey, look at me, but old things reach out and whisper to you. You have to lean in and listen, and then, that's when you can really take a good look. It warms my heart to see you kept so many old things. I bet your mom and dad are proud."

Her words bought tears to my eyes, and I hugged her, a brief squeeze around the shoulders. She patted my arm. "I'm glad you're living here, Christiana. I think this place will be good to you."

"Now that I have kitchen, I'll have you and Celeste over for home-made Sunday gravy, just like my grandmother made."

"We'll bring dessert. I found us a place, very nice. There's a kitchen we can use. It's very small, but then, our apartment wasn't such a grand space."

"What will you do, Celeste?" I asked her. "I know you loved working. Won't you miss all the people?"

She shrugged. "I'll meet new people. Just like you're doing." She waggled her finger at me, her nails painted a bright red. "It's never too late, you know that. Especially for us women. We're good at starting over."

I followed her outside, then went back to the front porch to greet more guests. Olivia Kopecknie arrived, the blonde that had danced with Craig Ferris at the pier all those weeks ago. I'd seen her around town, of course. She was hard to miss. She introduced herself, shaking my hand warmly.

"I hope you don't mind us popping in," she gushed. "I just heard so much about the house."

"Go on through," I told her. "And there's sandwiches and salads out back."

She introduced the good-looking man she was with as Ken Malcolm, and she clung to him the way her capris clung to her curves. Daniel and Marie arrived together, looking, once again, like a couple in an advertisement for a luxury resort. Daniel kissed my cheek. "Please tell me there's Stoli," he asked.

I shook my head. "Daniel, I no longer have to cater to your every whim, remember? But there's a keg out back."

Marie lifted her tote bag. "Not to worry," she purred. "As long as there's ice, we can make our own."

I shook my finger at her. "Don't start to spoil him, Marie."

She shrugged. "I won't. But I have to admit, this is great vodka."

Jenna and Craig Ferris arrived together. I was so happy for them. I'd gotten bits and pieces of their story from Terri and was glad they'd managed to find their way.

I stayed on the porch, basically directing traffic, so I wasn't close enough to hear what was said when Jenna cornered Olivia Kopecknie, but from the fire in Jenna's eyes I had a feeling Olivia was getting an earful. When Jenna came out on the porch, though, she seemed relaxed and happy.

"I'm glad to see you so happy, Jenna," I told her. "Craig is so great. You and he...fit together."

She smiled. "Yes, as a matter of fact, we do. Now, what about you and Mike McCann?"

I felt myself grin. I couldn't help it. It pretty much happened anytime anyone mentioned his name. "We're exploring possibilities."

"That's good. That's very good. Mike seems a good guy."

"He is. I'm not so sure about his brother." I stopped.

Terri had become friendlier to him, and I could see through their body language that she was moving closer to him and wanting physical intimacy. I couldn't blame her. I could also see that she was beginning to care for him as a person, and not just an idea. I remembered the few things that Mike had said about him and hoped that once the choice was made, things between them wouldn't fall apart.

"I think Terri is going to end up disappointed," I said.

"Terri is a big girl," Jenna said. "She knows what she's getting herself into."

She was right. I'd been saying the same thing all along. But still... "I guess. My only regret is that I never had a chance to have breakfast with all you single ladies."

Jenna frowned "I can't imagine giving them up," she said slowly. "We may have to expand our breakfast club requirements to include the newly deliriously attached."

I laughed. "Deliriously attached? I love that! Yes, I think I'd fit right in."

At that moment, Craig came out and put his arm around her shoulder, and she looked just as happy as I felt.

At some point during the day, I thought I'd stop smiling, but I was carried along by so many things: my house, finally done; my friends, relaxed and enjoying themselves: and Celeste and Connie, holding court in my patio and knowing they were looking forward to the future as well. And Mike. Every time I looked at him I felt like I was going to burst.

Miss Ava came over, walked through my house, and smiled her approval. "You will be a good neighbor," she said.

"How can you tell?" I asked.

"Because I can see how much this place means to you." She watched Joe as he came up on the porch to drink from his water bowl. "You better not let that dog bother Bella," she said sternly.

I laughed. "He's been chasing every squirrel he sees for weeks now. Luckily, he can't climb trees. Bella is safe, and as long as I'm living here, she'll remain safe." I explained Mike's idea that the town would buy the lot once Bella's status was established. "Celeste and Connie will donate the money to the town so Bella can remain exactly where she is."

Miss Ava smiled. "See? You *are* a good neighbor. Bella is lucky too."

At the end of the day, all my friends stayed to help clean up.

"After all," Stella said, "you have work tomorrow."

"So do you all," I said. "But thanks. And take this food. There's so much left over!"

Containers were wrapped and the brand new dishwasher was loaded, and I lit candles on the porch and sat with Mike.

"Any drunks come by yet?" He asked.

I shook my head. "No. Well, yes, but they just wave. Nobody's fallen asleep on the lawn or puked anywhere."

Joe, at his feet, yawned.

"He's had a hard day," I said.

Mike made a face. "And he managed to beg food from every person here. He's gonna get fat.'"

I took his hand and held it to my cheek. "It was a wonderful day," I said quietly.

He nodded. "I think you're going to be happy here, Chris."

"Yes." I kissed his palm. "You're a big part of that, you know."

He shook his head. "It's not me. It's us. *We're* a big part of it. We're lucky."

I nodded. The big gamble had paid off. Everything I'd done, all the chances I'd taken had gotten me to this one place, this one point in time where I felt a sense of belonging, of happiness, and of being at peace with myself.

Lucky indeed.

Chapter Eleven

I woke early Monday morning and felt the weight of Joe sleeping against my feet. Mike had not stayed the night. He had an early morning meeting with another client, a house on the water up near Silver Beach. I let Joe out and he ran over to the empty lot, sniffed around, and lifted his leg against every tree trunk. I called him in, fed him and got ready for work.

My hours were perfect—eight in the morning until two in the afternoon. I came home mentally exhausted. I hadn't been using that part of my brain for a while and was feeling slightly overwhelmed, but by mid-week I started to get a handle on how things were done. The young woman I was replacing was hugely pregnant and constantly running to the bathroom, but she was smart and well organized and a patient teacher. The job and I were going to get along just fine.

Joe spent a couple of days at the house that first week with me and was settling in just fine.

"He likes it better here," Mike said.

"I doubt it. I'm just home more. And he likes to watch for Bella." We were sitting on the porch, and I reached into my pocket and handed him a key. "In case you want to drop him off and I'm not home.

I'd hate to think of him across the street with all that noise going on. You know you can bring him over any time, right?"

He looked at the key and then lifted his eyes to mine. "Thank you. This means a lot."

"Well I know you're a love-me-love-my-dog kind of guy."

His gaze never wavered. "Yes. That I am."

I could feel the weight of words hanging between us, but I tore my eyes away. "Breakfast club this Saturday morning. Be warned. I won't be around."

"Breakfast club? Is that really a thing?"

I nodded. "Jenna and Karen and Stella and Terri and Marie. Every Saturday morning at the Town Pharmacy. It started out as a single ladies kind of thing, but they've opened up their membership."

He chuckled. "Just an excuse to gather around and cluck like a bunch of hens."

I nodded. "Yes. And I can't wait."

"Well, when you get around to talking about me, go easy, okay?"

"Why, Mike. I can't think of a single negative thing I could say about you," I said, covering my heart with both hands.

He snickered. "Well that's because we're still in whatchacall the honeymoon phase. Wait a few more months when I start belching and scratching myself at the breakfast table."

I started to laugh. "Oh?"

"And when football season starts, well, forget about Sunday afternoons. Or Monday nights. Or any other day or evening there's game."

I rolled my eyes. "Oh, please, Mike. Tell me it ain't so."

He stretched out his legs, grinning. "And did I mention my chili? I make a big pot every Friday night once the weather turns, and I eat it all week long. The farts are incredible."

I was laughing so hard there were tears in my eyes.

"But on the other hand," he continued, his eyes twinkling, "I'm pretty good in the sack, so you be sure to mention that when you start listing all my sins."

I shook my head. "Mike, I think I'd just as soon keep all your sins to myself."

He waved a hand. "Nah. Just wait. Cause I know you all won't be swapping recipes." He clasped his hands across his chest. "I think Daniel is developing quite a fondness for Marie."

I raised an eyebrow. "Oh? So do *you* sit around and cluck like a bunch of hens?"

He shook his head. "Nope, we crow like roosters."

I waited a beat. "What about Steve? Does he say anything about Terri."

He crossed his ankles. "You talk to her lately?"

"Not since the party. Why?"

"Well. Apparently they've finally gone and done the deed."

I felt a slow, sinking feeling in my chest. "Oh?"

He sighed. "My brother, well, he liked the chase. Or, rather, he liked being chased. She played the whole thing pretty smart, I think."

"But now?"

He shrugged. "Steve...he spent most of his life chasing me, thinking he needed to have whatever I had, but more. Or bigger. Or better. When I told him about you and I, I think he looked around and saw Terri and figured she was smart and attractive, and the fact that she wasn't falling all over him, well, she piqued his interest. But he's just not a guy for the long haul. Never has been."

I sighed. "That's too bad. I think she was starting to like him, not just...want him."

He leaned his head back. "He's always just taken what he wanted, but he's older now, maybe wiser. If she's smart, she won't tell him that he's the best thing she's ever had. Maybe if he comes back to her enough, he'll find something in her that he *needs*. Men don't like to admit they need things." He reached over with his foot and nudged mine. "I need you," he said quietly.

I felt my heart beat faster. "That's good to hear," I said lightly, not wanting to give away too much. I didn't tell him how much I needed him, his strength and calm, his humor and kindness. I didn't tell him how much he added to my life, to my everyday happiness. But maybe now is the moment, I thought, and I took a breath. Maybe now I take another giant step...

"Well, I've got to be back up Silver Beach in the morning," he said. "How about you forgo your usual Friday night festivities and go fishing with me tomorrow evening? We can leave around six, stay out a few hours, catch the sunset?"

The moment was gone. "Fishing? As in, picking up something and impaling it on a sharp hook, and then..."

He stood up and laughed. "No, I'll do all that. You can hold the fishing pole, though, and if you get a bite, I'll help you reel it in, and I'll even cook it right here on your grill out back."

I stood and kissed him lightly. "Deal."

I walked him out to the back, where his truck was parked next to my car, right beside the patio. Joe jumped in the front seat and Mike waved as they pulled away.

"I love you," I said softly as I watched them go.

I'd been in the Town Pharmacy before, of course. It was the only drug store for miles around. When I walked in the following Saturday morning with Terri, four faces looked up, surprised. But only for a second.

Stella jumped up and pulled a chair in from a neighboring table. "Wendy," she called, "looks like we need another setup."

I stopped short. "I hope you all don't mind," I said. "It was Jenna who invited me."

Jenna nodded. "That's right. Since I'm not, technically, a single lady anymore, and neither is Stella, I thought we could expand our membership to include...the what did I say? The deliriously attached?"

The waitress appeared with a coffee mug and silverware. "I'm Wendy," she said. "Are you going to be a regular here? It's fine, but we may have to move you all to the table by the window. It's bigger."

"We've been at this table for years, Wendy." Marie said. "It's quite big enough."

Wendy shrugged. "These ladies usually don't need a menu," she said, going back to the front counter and returning with a simple laminated sheet. "We're pretty basic here, but if you don't see what you want, ask. We're pretty flexible."

I sat and looked at the menu. As I read, the other ladies all said the same thing: the usual. I chose carefully, so that some day in the near future I could also say, the usual, and it would be something I wouldn't get tired of.

"Blueberry pancakes. A short stack, please. And crispy bacon." I handed Wendy the menu and she was gone.

"So," Karen said, stirring her coffee. "How was your first week of work?"

I took a sip. The coffee was delicious. If the pancakes were half as good... "It's a lot to learn, but so far, so good. I think I'm going to like it there. The people are all very friendly, and I can't beat the hours."

Jenna leaned forward. "I'm kinda sorta thinking about applying there myself, just to be closer to home."

Marie arched her eyebrow. "Getting domesticated, I see. Well, it's about time you settled in. I'm so glad that Craig came with a ready-made family. Is he keeping Sam's on Main?"

Jenna shook her head and began to talk about an arrangement Craig had made with Glory, the woman who was the cook there. I kept glancing at Terri, wondering if she was going to say anything about Steve. She kept her eyes down.

Stella cleared her throat. "I want to know about this Daniel person. You and he looked very comfortable at Chris's party last weekend. Yes, Marie, I am talking about you. Don't look like there's somebody *else* he showed up with."

Marie pointed at me. "She can tell you much more about Daniel than I can.'"

"True," I said. "But my information is a year out of date."

Marie looked thoughtful. "He's complicated," she said at last. "And charming. Very smart, and an excellent businessman. He has much too high an opinion of himself and hates to let anyone see his softer side. I imagine he's very generous and thoughtful around people he cares about, but he likes to let everyone think he has a heart of stone."

I laughed. "Well, how about that? Sounds just like the old Daniel."

Her face softened. "The Main Street project will be done in a few months, then he's going back up to Rehoboth to finish up something *there* before starting the medical park. Actual construction is months away, but he'll be back down here after the first of the year for a bit. Permits and zoning changes will take up most of his time.

Lucky for him, he's got a first-class attorney working with him on that."

Stella beamed. "Well, good for you. I have to say, I talked to him a bit at Chris', and he *was* charming. A bit of a flirt, too."

"Yes," Marie said. "That he is."

"And you, Terri," Karen said. "You and Steve seem to be getting along fairly well. How's that going? Anything new to report?"

Terri shook her head. "No. I'm taking my advice from Chris here, and remaining interested but aloof."

I looked down into my coffee. Either Steve had lied to Mike about the two of them, or Terri knew she'd blundered.

The conversation drifted after that. The pancakes were delicious, and so was the second cup of coffee, and finally Terri and I walked back up Main Street. It was noisy and quite crowded, even as far down as my house.

She came up on the porch and looked up and down the street. "Another two or three weeks, and we'll be back to normal," she said. "Nice and quiet. No cars, no strangers, no noise."

"And nobody threw up in my yard."

She snorted. "We still have a few weeks to go. Listen, I found another house. In Eastville. Want to come out and see it on Sunday? With Steve?"

I looked over at her. "What's going on with you two?"

She looked over at Miss Ava's yard. "I finally issued an invitation and he accepted," she said.

I kept quiet.

"And I can safely say that all of the rumors about his prowess are true."

"Well," I said. "Congratulations, I guess. This is what you wanted, right?"

She shook her head. "In the beginning, yes. But I've been watching you and Mike, and that's what I *really* wanted. For Steve to look at me the way Mike looks at you." Her voice cracked. "And I really like him, Chris, now that I've gotten to know him. He's not just this handsome, sexy guy. I thought that we were working toward something."

"But?" I asked, gently.

"But I haven't heard from him since Sunday night. Well, Monday morning. He just…left. That's it. A real dick move."

I felt so badly for her. "Oh, Terri, honey I'm sorry."

She shook her head and I could see tears glistening in her eyes. "I don't know why I was stupid enough to think that I was any different than all those other women. Because I did think that. I kept him at arms length and I thought that would make a difference. But I don't think it's in him to want to stay. He's not like Mike."

"No," I said softly. "He's not."

She looked at me. "Are you in love with him?"

I nodded. "Yes."

"Have you told him?"

I shook my head. "No."

"Why not?"

"I don't want to spoil this."

She leaned forward. "Chris, look how far you've come this summer. Look at what you've done. You've built yourself a home, you've stepped in and made a difference in those two old ladies' lives, you've even managed to make yourself a first-class enemy. And this from the woman who a few years ago was afraid to stand up for anything because she was too afraid of rocking the boat. Tell him. Because I bet he feels the same way."

I swallowed hard. "Maybe."

"Not maybe. For sure." She stood up abruptly. "What about the house?"

"You know, I'm not sure that Steve and Mike can help us with another project. I know that Mike has been up to Silver Beach a few times, and with the medical park next year…"

Terri looked down at her feet and shrugged. "Just as well, I guess. Working with Steve might be awkward."

I stood up and hugged her. "Terri, maybe he'll realize what a wonderful person you are, and what a jerk he's been. He can come around."

She shook her head. "No. And I don't think I could have done anything differently. He just…well, he is who he is, and he's obviously not for me." She went down the walk and headed to her place. I sat back down and closed my eyes, feeling an ache for her.

Daniel invited me to have dinner with him and Celeste and Connie to celebrate the sale of their property. We ate at a small place up the highway, close to where the two sisters were going to be living. The inventory had been removed in the previous weeks, and Daniel described the huge shell of the Coop, empty and dark. Celeste rolled her eyes.

"Thank God I'll never have to worry about sweeping that barn of a place again," she said

Connie smiled. "Somebody does all the cleaning at our new place," she said happily. "And there are ducks across the street. Celeste wheels me out every morning."

Celeste poked Daniel with her elbow. "Make sure whoever plans out your assisted living facility that there are ground floor units. We want to be able to just step outside whenever we want."

Daniel cracked a smile. "Of course."

"And make sure there's a good-sized community kitchen," Connie said. "This place we're in now doesn't allow for a bunch of us to get together and cook."

"And maybe a wading pool?" Celeste suggested.

Daniel's smile broadened. "Why don't you two just sit down with the architects yourselves?" he joked.

Celeste, however, nodded seriously. "That's a very good idea," she said. "Please set that up for us."

Daniel looked taken aback, then laughed. "Done, ladies. Done."

It was a good dinner, and Daniel drove me back to my house, dropping me off.

"Things are good?" he asked.

I nodded. "Yes. You and Marie are coming next week?" I had already had Celeste and Connie over for a long, happy Sunday dinner but planned a potluck for all my friends the next week.

"Of course. She's bringing what she calls her world famous dumplings, and I'll bring my world famous cocktail shaker and a gallon of Stoli. We're both looking forward to it."

"I'm happy for you. Listen, I want you to know that when we were together, I was very..."

"You were content," he said. "As was I. We made an excellent couple because we were both what the other needed at the time."

"Yes." I said.

"And because we're both probably happier now doesn't take anything away from that."

"No. It doesn't. And I'm glad you're with Marie, and I hope she's what you want right now."

He rolled his eyes. "Please, do not get sentimental."

"Of course not, Daniel. But still...I like Marie a lot."

He flashed a smile. "So do I." He looked at me. "You seem much happier here."

"I am."

"I'm glad. And you do seem...braver. This whole thing of yours to take more risks has appeared to have made a real difference."

"I think it has. I'm not sure I'd be where I am right now if I hadn't been willing to put myself out there."

"You mean with Mike?"

I nodded. "And with Celeste and Connie. Can you imagine me, a year ago, risking so much on the word of a little old lady who swore there was a super-squirrel living next door?"

He made a face. "Well you don't quite know if that's paid off or not. What if Bella decides on her own to leave town?"

"Then I lose. But I don't think I will."

"I don't think you will either." He leaned over and gave me a quick kiss on the cheek. "Good night."

I went inside, lit a few candles, and stretched out on the couch. I was happy. I felt as though everything I'd been looking for had all come together in a perfect whole.

It didn't get cold on the Eastern Shore, not *really* cold, or so everyone told me. But somewhere in the middle of October, the air took on a chill and the leaves started to turn, and the long, glorious summer was over.

The building across the street was complete and had been fully leased. Yes, there was a bank, a young couple that made their own bagels, a dry cleaner and a bookstore. I was quite happy.

Mike didn't drop Joe off in the mornings anymore, but when he stayed over, Joe spent the next day. We had fallen into a pattern of quiet, happy rituals: Sunday morning omelets, Wednesday night binge watching old Seinfeld episodes, Saturday afternoon antique hunting. He was still playful, kind, and ardent. His touch still sent shivers to all the right places. Sunday afternoons, while he watched football, Terri and I shopped or saw a movie.

"Has he told you that he loves you yet?" She would ask.

I'd shake my head and roll my eyes. "We're not teenagers, Terri. I know how important I am to him, just as he knows what he means to me. I don't need words."

And I didn't. But I would have liked to hear them.

Amy McCann purchased the lot next door, and Dr. Ava Wilson filed an affidavit with the town, the county, and the State Fish and Wildlife Department. I sat and waited to see what Amy's next move would be. According to Marie, she had not filed any plans or proposals with the town, but she also knew about the little squirrel living next door to me, what she was and what that meant.

She pulled up in front of the house in the early evening during a brief Indian Summer, when the temperatures had soared up past eighty, and Mike and I were out on the porch. There was very little traffic to watch now, but we liked to watch the customers going in and out of the book store, and guess what they had just bought.

"Now, there's a Stephen King fan right there. I bet he just bought his eleventh copy of *It*," Mike said.

"Why on earth would he need eleven copies?"

"Different covers. You don't know those horror aficionados."

"And you do?"

"I'll have you know I've seen *Friday the 13th* almost thirty times."

"Almost?"

"Well, I fell asleep during some of them, so you can't count them as a whole, you see."

I laughed. He could always make me laugh.

A sleek Mercedes pulled up to the curb, and Mike made a noise. Joe lifted his head and growled, low in his throat.

"Who..?" I stood up and watched as Amy McCann came briskly up my walk.

She stopped short and stared. "Mike? What the hell are you doing here?"

Mike smiled. "I hang out here a lot."

She looked at me, then back at him, and a sly, quite unpleasant smile came to her ace. "A happy couple? I see. Well, now, isn't that just so romantic."

I crossed my arms and went down a step. "Are you here for a specific reason, Amy, or just stopping by to say hello?"

She adjusted the large tote bag on her arm. "Your neighbor has filed with the town that there's a rare and endangered animal nesting in the lot next door, and the town seems very reluctant to allow me to build."

"Oh? How about that."

She took a step closer. "Listen. You were in real estate. You know how hard it is, especially if you're a woman. And believe me, I've been fighting the boy's club around here for years." She lowered her voice, just us girls. "I really wouldn't build a fourteen unit anything here, it just wouldn't make sense. But I've got to do something. What would make you happy, Chris? A nice, little single family? I could build something similar to your house, it would be quite lovely."

"You seem to think that I have some sort of power in this situation, Amy. I don't know why you would think that. A very well respected expert has sworn that an endangered animal has somehow decided to nest in, well, *your* trees. I can't help that. I can't help it if the town has decided not to go to battle with the State Wildlife Commission over it."

She smiled. "Come on, give me a break here. I paid a lot of money for that piece of property."

"Because you thought you could use it to get what you wanted from Connie and Celeste Montecorvo. And that was the only reason. Do I look stupid to you, Amy?" I heard Mike behind me shift in his chair, Joe was silent.

Her eyes narrowed. "You lied to me about that whole thing."

"And?"

She stepped back. "What do you mean *and?*"

"I didn't lie to you. I just played around with words, and you drew your own conclusions. But if I did lie, I certainly wouldn't feel guilty about it. My loyalty is with Celeste, not you."

I saw the anger in her eyes and it was, I admit, rather intimidating. She stepped forward, then leaned toward me. "I can fight this, you know that damn squirrel isn't on the federal list, you know."

"Yes, I know. The Commonwealth of Virginia still has a pretty high opinion of her, though. Fight away."

"It will cost you money."

"No, It won't. I'm not the town, or the state, or even a conservation group from Delaware that's perfectly prepared to have its members lie down in front of bulldozers if need be. This will, however, cost *you* money. How much are you willing to spend for spite?"

She looked past me at Mike and practically snarled. "You think you have friends here? Well, so do I, and let me tell you—"

I heard Mike walk down the porch steps and felt him come up behind me. His arm went across my shoulder and he pulled me close.

"I'd be careful here, Amy. This happens to be the woman I love, and I wouldn't take very kindly to any of your usual dirt spilling onto her. You really don't have as many friends as you think, and I you might remember the last time you thought you could throw your weight around. It didn't go over too well in this town."

My throat was suddenly dry and I swear my heart was pounding so hard that I thought I would explode.

A look flickered across her face and I saw her withdraw. "You two deserve each other," she snarled.

I felt the tension leave my body. She was done. "Why, thank you, Amy. I think so too."

She turned and clattered back to her car on spiked heels, her whole body trembling with anger. She slammed the door of her car shut, loudly, and sped down Main Street.

I was still standing, Mike beside me. He slipped both his arms across my chest and I felt his breath in my ear. "I know. You don't need rescuing. I just couldn't stand by and let her, well—"

"No. It was...fine. Thank you." My mouth was dry and my voice cracked. He'd said it. He said the words, I'd heard them, but was it a show for Amy? Or was I really the woman he loved. Was it worth asking? What if..?"

"Did you mean it?"

His hands rubbed my shoulders and I felt his lips in my hair. "Of course I meant it. I won't let her start one of her nasty little campaigns against you. Why, I'll—"

"No," I broke in. "I meant the part about being the woman you love?"

He was very still, and then he turned me around and looked down at me, his eyes steady and warm. "Of course I love you, Chris. Have from just about the first time I saw you. I know I haven't said it, and I probably should have. I love you and I am grateful every day that you think I deserve a place in your world." He kissed me on the forehead. "And I just hope that you'll love me too, one of these days. I can be an awful fool about some things, but I promise, if you give me enough time, well, I'll kinda grow on you."

I drew back and pushed him, hard. "You idiot," I yelled. "You complete idiot."

He stepped back, looking stunned. "Oh, God, I've done it now, haven't I? Listen, Chris—"

I reached up and threw my arms around his neck, covering his mouth and cutting off his words.

He finally drew back and looked down at me, eyes twinkling. "Well, I did kinda hope," he said.

"I love you like crazy. I love you like, like..."

"I believe you."

Joe suddenly sprang off the porch and dashed into the lot next door and I saw her, Bella, a flash of silver racing across the ground and disappearing up the trunk and into the pine branches. Joe circled the tree, barking.

"There's my girl," I said.

"That's her? She's a beauty."

"Yes, she certainly is."

"And I've never seen any one person get so excited about seeing a squirrel run up a tree."

"Not any squirrel," I said. "That's Bella."

Joe sat beneath the tree, looking up

"Always hopeful," Mike cracked, then laughed. "Come on, Joe. We've got everything we need right here," he called.

Joe gave a final, wistful look, then scampered back and followed us as we went up the steps and home.

Also by Dee Ernst

Stealing Jason Wilde

Am I Zen Yet?

Better Than Your Dreams

A Slight Change of Plan

A Different Kind of Forever

Better Off Without Him

The Mt. Abrams Mysteries

A Mother's Day Murder

A Founders' Day Death

A Killer Halloween

A Deadly New Year

A Malicious Midwinter

A Fatal April Shower

The Eastern Shore Romances

A Safe Place to Land

Building Home